DEBRA ANASTASIA

DEDICATION

For T, D, and J
This one is for you, too. #12

Acknowledgements

Husband and Kids: You are my happy bubble.

Helena: Pepper loves Salt

Tijan: I love our visits all the damn time!

Nina: #NinaReadPough

Teresa: We can do this!

Erika: I love how you welcome my crazy.

Jillian: You rock

Texas K: Thanks for all the support on the crapper

Pam: I'll see you on Sunday nights

Jen Matera: Still sorry about that Fire book.

Pam Brooks—Radio Genius

Tara S and Meghan: Sweet Jesus. I love you.

Beverly C, Nise, Patti, Michele, Nancee, Daisy, Liv and Ruth

Mom and Dad (S&D) Uncle Ted and Aunt Jo: I can't wait to see you in Florida

PST girls forever! Thanks to my boob group, all the Pams, the Filets, 101, C.O.P.A and all the FB groups that offer so much help.

CP Smith for the ADORABLE insides!

My SWAT Team and the Revenger Group!

Heather Wish, Dina Littner, L.J. Lisa, Roberta Curry, Ramona Johnson, Eve Chin Lavin, Blair Ackerman, Robyn Diebolt and TL wainwright Lisa S.

Friends, family, readers, bloggers and author friends – Thank you!

My Beautiful Booty Camp Review Stars:

Heather C. Leigh
Paula Radell
Katherine Stevens
Tara Sivec
Meghan Quinn
Mella from Lu's Buchgeflüster
Elaine from Beyond Books
Ella Fox
Sara Celi
Crissy Maier
CL Sayers
Nancee Cain
Lauren Rosa
Christina Santos
Erika L. James
Liv Morris
Jiffy Kate
SM Lumetta
Teresa Mummert
Helena Hunting

My beta team:
Lauren Rosa
Christina Santos
Angelica Maria Quintero
Ciara Hunter
Sarah Piechuta
Elaine Turner
Michele MacLoed
Eve Chin Lavin

CI♥WN FETISH

Hazel's throat was raw from screaming Scott's name. He did that to her. With his hands, his mouth, and his long, thin penis. She was lying on a towel which was wet enough to have soaked through to the mattress below. His sexual talents made her feel more beautiful than she'd ever felt before. Her eyes stayed closed, but she heard him rustling around. Her fingertips felt like rubber. Hazel touched the pad of her index finger to the nail on her thumb. He'd fucked the feeling out of her hands. She could sleep like this, splayed out on the bed, naked and rosy. She was betting her nipples were a hot red and might even match the marks he'd left on her ass cheeks.

Maybe even the blush on her face would match, too, as she thought of how, in between screaming his name, God's name, and a lot of guttural sounds, she'd told him she loved him.

That was not a step she'd planned to take while her ankles were on his shoulders, but when her body had been strung tight like a fist and he'd released it with a combo that should be in every boyfriend handbook, Hazel's mouth made its own decisions.

Scott was taking longer than he should have to bring back a warm, wet towel from the bathroom, so she forced herself to peel open at least one eyelid to check on him.

He was buttoning his jeans.

Hazel let herself enjoy the sight of him—the bare chest and jeans was a classic combo, and he made it look good. She finally made it to his face and offered him a satisfied smile—he sure as hell had earned it.

Scott was stone-faced.

"You okay?" She was so boneless she couldn't even move yet, so her concern was only on her tongue.

"I'm leaving." He pulled his T-shirt over his head.

"Oh? Are you hungry? I can make something. I know you've got nothing to cook upstairs." She let her hand flop onto her stomach.

Just as she was thinking about how lovely it was that they were so comfortable naked with each other, he changed the atmosphere in the entire room. "No, I'm leaving you. This is over. I'm done."

Now Hazel was able to prop up on an elbow. Though the words were confusing and her brain was trying to wrap around what he'd said, it was his flat tone that had her heart pounding all over again—but for different reasons.

"You're going back to your apartment?"

The room's scent was so hardwired into her brain—telling her she was happy—that she just couldn't make the connections she needed to.

"I'm breaking up with you right now."

Hazel finally sat all the way up. "What?"

Scott was fully clothed now but picking up his shoes

because apparently he was in such a rush that he couldn't take the time to put them on. Scott was at her bedroom door before he looked back over his shoulder.

She was in midcrouch now, trying to gather her clothes. He took one last look at her naked, bent form.

"That last orgasm was my parting gift. I've got another girl. She lives on the top floor of this apartment. Don't make this weird for me, okay?"

Scott closed the bedroom door, and she sat on the floor, holding her pants and one sock. It took him a few minutes to close the front door. Later, she would figure out that he'd stopped to take the six-pack of beer he'd stashed in her fridge while they fucked.

And that's what they'd done. Scott had changed it on her, from making love to fucking.

It had been the first time she'd ever told a guy that she loved them.

And as she hugged her two articles of clothing to her chest, she promised herself it would be the last.

XⴲXⴲXⴲXⴲ

It wasn't until he was drilling his new girlfriend on her ceiling that she realized she needed to move out of her apartment. Well, it wasn't really on her ceiling, but on his floor that also happened to be her ceiling. No amount of screaming, loud music, or broom handle banging would make him stop. Or her. The new girlfriend had a super annoying habit. The harder she came, the harder she laughed. The shrill sound of her explosive laughter as Scott made every sex dream she'd ever had come true induced nightmares for Hazel. Very specific nightmares involving clowns in fetish gear.

She had to move. She had to get out.

It wasn't so easy to get the hell out of a one-year lease, and in her panic, Hazel had a moment of extreme insanity. Well, maybe it was a sleep-deprived decision made in anger and sadness. And a severe desire to be out from under Scott's hyena-pounding. When her best friend, Claire called screaming about winning a chance to be a part of Booty Camp, Hazel allowed herself to be swept away in her friend's excitement.

Booty Camp
Dating Service

Hazel Lavender gave her best friend, Claire Paquet, a hard look after she got the receipt from the car service driver.

"If my tits pop out of this top one more time, you owe me your firstborn child."

Claire patted the tops of her boobs like they were friendly pets. "Stay puppies. Good job." Then she turned her attention back to Hazel's face with some advice. "Just don't do any whore bends and you'll be fine."

Claire could convince a fish in a bowl to buy a bottle of water. Her friend's powers of persuasion had brought them to the front doors of the old movie theater downtown. Hazel wished the wine bottle they'd polished off at Claire's apartment while getting dressed had provided bravado with more staying power.

But all it had done was given her the courage to jam her breasts into a top owned by the slightly less-endowed Claire and call it sufficient.

But what do you wear to meet the love of your life?

That was the question the wine had answered.

The answer was a swishy skirt, a titty top, and high heels.

No jacket required.

As the chill from the evening breeze swept over her chest, Hazel seriously doubted the alcohol's qualifications to make that decision. Although she *was* enjoying feeling carefree and not giving a moment's thought to Scott and his upstairs hyena.

There was a single sign on the glass doors leading to the venue.

WELCOME TO BOOTY CAMP DATING SERVICE!

Claire pointed at it. "Well, we're in the right spot. Are you ready to fall in hopeless, orgasmic love?"

"It's convoluted. Like the Emperor's new clothes. This is a horrible idea, and you hate me." Hazel concentrated on getting up the cement stairs without falling. The whole building seemed like it had come from another time when everything was smaller. Dinner plates, drinks, and— apparently—stairs. There was a generous wheelchair ramp to the left of the entrance, and Hazel couldn't have been happier to see it there. She always noted when vintage buildings successfully retro-fitted their accessibility options.

She sucked at heels. She so rarely wore them to work, but her tormentor/boss/best friend was smooth in them. Claire even had a pair of high-heeled sneakers. Now, she didn't wear them, but the fact that they existed and Claire felt compelled to own them really highlighted the differences in their personalities. And jobs.

Hazel was a third-year special education teacher, and Claire was her assistant principal. Claire was the perfect remedy to a soggy heart that had been screwed over too hard by Scott.

They had met at the pool back home years ago. Claire was six years older and had been the college-aged pool manager when Hazel arrived there for her very first job. They'd hit it off despite the gap in their ages.

But now, hurrying into the lobby of the theater to avoid the crisp breeze, they were far from the hot summer days of years ago.

Everyone in the lobby glanced over in the city way of checking them out without appearing to check them out. Hazel smoothed down the back of Claire's bright red hair where the elements had mussed it up.

Claire was talking to someone right off. She was just outgoing. And when she was nervous, she was even more outgoing. Hazel pulled her phone out of her purse and held it like a lifeline.

The room was full of single people looking for a connection. It felt like an odd mixture of *being* the steak fed to a group of sharks and fighting to get the last clearance dress at a sample sale. The competition and the want in the room were thick.

Smiling, attractive people wearing black T-shirts with "Booty Camp" emblazoned on them worked the room, holding out clipboards and pens.

Hazel looked at Claire as the tall, dark, and handsome Booty Camp Dating Service employee handed her two clipboards. She thanked him distractedly and narrowed her eyes at Claire when she placed her hand on the man's forearm.

It was the hook-up gesture. Hazel had been in too many bars when Claire was PMS-horny not to notice it was her signature move.

If Claire was really into the guy, she would comment on the strength and squeeze.

"Do you lift? My heavens, these are some firm muscles right here."

Bingo.

Hazel was too intimidated to glance around again. She started filling out her permission form, as it were. She added the usual: her name, number, and profession. There were no leading questions. She expected a ream of paper that grilled her on egg preference and her favorite bands, but instead, Booty Camp got right to the good part—writing out a check. She could have swiped her card on the payment square each Booty Camp employee had on their phones, but Hazel's father's distrust of all cellular devices and scams made her decide to go the paper route.

One thousand dollars. She gave Claire the evil eye that the woman missed. Hazel made out her check grandma style and clipped it to the board before passing it back to the smiley Booty Camp girl who introduced herself as Alison. The staff member had a fancy camera that printed out an instant candid snap of Hazel, and she clipped that to the board before it had even developed.

At this point, Claire was flat-out canoodling. Hazel had never seen anything that would fit the definition before in person, but Claire had her boobs propped up like two parrots on the guy's forearm while fluttering her eyelashes. Said guy was built—tall and looked a lot like Gaston from "Beauty and the Beast." He was the exact opposite of Claire's type. She was always looking for waiflike, pained blond dudes. This guy was masculine with a capital Balls.

Hazel felt her jaw drop when Gaston waved away the Booty Camp girl as she tried to give Claire a clipboard. "This one is comped." He smoldered at Claire like they were both wearing matching satin jock shorts.

Her assistant principal best friend, who handled just about any human with an efficient business tone, giggled like she was getting her armpits tickled. When Gaston sidled closer to swing his giant arm around Claire's shoulders, Hazel saw he had the company logo on the back of his shirt, as well.

Claire's happy gaze fell on Hazel's face. Her friend mimicked grabbing Gaston's ass but stopped just short of doing so to show Hazel how interested she was in the man.

Hazel raised her eyebrows in acknowledgment. Claire always excelled. She was a driven lady. And if the goal was to get a man, well, it shouldn't surprise Hazel that Claire had completed the goal before she was even officially registered—and with an employee, no less.

Hazel looked around the room. All the people were fairly typical of those she would meet out on a Friday night. They were stylish and corporate-looking.

On the perimeter of the lobby, she spotted a guy who made her feel something other than awkward embarrassment. Now he was mouth-wateringly hot. Clearly he didn't belong—with his longish hair and high cheekbones. Even all the way across the room, she could tell his eyes were a piercing, hot blue. He was either wearing guyliner and mascara or he had the kind of eyelashes that made every lady grit her teeth in jealously. When he turned a little, she saw that he was wearing a shirt that matched Gaston's.

Hazel wanted to roll her eyes, but instead Claire caught her by her upper arms and shook her.

"I bet his man salami is like a fist!" Claire was flushed and her eyes were sparkling.

"If you tell me you're in love, I'm going to punch you in the vagina."

"I'm in love."

"Son of a bitch."

Claire started filling Hazel in on all the details she'd been able to glean from Gaston during their four-minute relationship, but Hazel tuned her out and peered over her shoulder.

Guyliner was making his way over to Gaston. She wanted to hear his voice. Not that she was checking him out—because she certainly wasn't.

His dark jeans and motorcycle boots were not similar to the other employees' attire. He was having some strong words with Gaston. Hazel tuned in and overheard:

"No dating clients. You know that."

The guyliner voice was sexy and low. However, the thick, dark smudges weren't guyliner, They were totally just the lashes that were brimming this guy's peepers.

"Have you heard a word I've said?" Claire waved her hands in front of Hazel's face.

Hazel grabbed them and held them. "No. I was eavesdropping."

Claire followed Hazel's gesture and saw Gaston and Dark Lashes having heated words. "I might have to write that up as some fanfiction with me in the middle."

Hazel laughed. "I think I'd read the hell out of that."

Dark Lashes stalked away, and Hazel got a glimpse of his tight ass. He even had a tattoo trailing up his forearm.

"You're checking him out, aren't ya?" Claire slipped her arm around Hazel's waist.

"I'm scoping this joint out so when they start swearing us in to the cult, I know how to get us out." Hazel wrapped her arm around Claire as well and felt the tips of her friend's long red hair brush her skin.

"So cynical. Seriously, we've watched the ads a million times. A hundred and ten percent guaranteed to find your soul mate. I mean, how can we not take the chance? Did I tell you that's his name, too? Chance." Claire wiggled the tips of her fingertips in Gaston's direction. He *would* be named Chance.

"I'm going to take a Chance right in the back of my throat if he gives a girl a shot. Damn. Have we ever met someone so incredibly big? He's like a house. Do you see the way his T-shirt looks like it's going to tear right off his goddamned body?"

Hazel tried to find Dark Lashes, but he was gone. Instead, she was meeting all kinds of inquisitive eyes from the other men in the lobby. It was a meat market.

"He should have gotten the next size up. One sneeze and he'll tear right out of his clothes."

"A girl can hope. Do you have pepper in your purse?" Claire seemed serious as she pawed at Hazel's bag.

"No. Stop. We have to listen." The teacher in Hazel insisted on paying attention when someone was trying to speak to a group.

When Claire saw that it was Chance clapping, she was instantly riveted and stopped trying to mug Hazel.

It took a few claps and a whistle or two, but eventually the singles were eyes forward.

"Welcome to Booty Camp Dating Service!" Chance totally defeated all his efforts to quiet the crowd with his boisterous greeting. The crowd hooted and clapped.

Booty Camp Dating Service was so aggressively advertised on TV, on social media, and on billboards it almost seemed like they were meeting a celebrity. Well, if the celebrity was a dating app. It toured the United States, and there had been a marked increase in births roughly nine months after they'd embarked on the first leg.

Despite the cheeky name, Booty Camp Dating Service had a stupidly fabulous reputation for matching singles with their forever person. It had reached epic proportions, especially with late-night TV doing skits about Booty Camp.

The classically opulent theater was a study in deep red velvets and gold trimmings. Booty Camp was in town for two months. And Booty Camp was expensive. After winning the ticket lotto —thanks to Claire for babysitting that process without saying a word—Hazel was rewarded with having to lay out a thousand dollars for the honor of becoming a coveted Booty Camp success story. A hundred and ten percent happy. That's what the ads all said, anyway.

Chance managed to get the crowd settled again.

"Congrats on your admission to the program! We're so successful because *you* will be successful. After you've been processed by one of our Booty professionals, please make your way into the screening room."

Quite a few girls around them were fanning their faces and sneaking snapshots on their phone of Chance beefcaking around. The doors were opened by Booty Camp counselors.

Dark Lashes was hanging back, and Hazel pretended to sweep her hair up to a ponytail and peeked over her shoulder at him at the same time.

He caught her eye and gave her a very fatherly wink. She bit her lip so she wouldn't frown.

Claire nudged her. "Let's go. I want to get a good seat. Why are you blushing?"

"No reason. This whole thing makes me self-conscious."

The theater was well-lit and had deep, velvet seats. The pushier among the group made their way to the front, closest to the stage and, therefore, the screen. It was as if these people thought getting the best seats would help them find their soul mates quicker. Hazel pulled on Claire's arm until they were in the center of the back row.

Claire wiggled in her seat when Chance found her and pointed at her from the stage where he now stood, holding a microphone. After everyone was seated and the excitement had died down, Chance stirred them up again.

"Your soul mate could be here. Right now." He motioned around the packed theater. "Look around. It's not uncommon for our Booty Camp clients to lock eyes right this moment with the person they'll marry in six months. So do it. Feel it."

Hazel could feel her eyes rolling, so she closed them in case—on some random chance—the man for her was here, his first vision of her wouldn't be filled with the sarcasm. It felt like a superstition or an exercise in fruition. But she didn't throw out a raffle ticket until the numbers were announced, either, so...

She looked over her shoulder and found herself staring at Dark Lashes. He didn't smile, and neither did she. He looked bored. Like just another day at the office, which she guessed it was for him as he sat in the back row adjacent to hers. Finally, he touched his temple with his index finger and pointed back at the crowd in front of them. It took her a minute to understand his sign language, but when she got it, she felt her cheeks flush. He wanted her to put her gaze forward. To stop looking at him.

She bit her bottom lip. What an asshole. What did he think—she was trying to tempt him into dating her?

Hazel gave him the middle finger and an exasperated look. He could jump to conclusions, but she wasn't here to try and snag a man. Well, she wouldn't mind finding a guy to take back to her apartment so Scott would have to step around them making out in front of the elevator. That would be some sweet revenge.

She gave Dark Lashes another hard look, and this time he seemed to be struggling with a smirk.

"Jerk," Hazel muttered.

"Who? Chance?" Claire was focused on the man on stage who was feeding the crowd some impossible statistics.

"Did you know that woman who are single after twenty-six are eighty-nine percent more likely to die alone than their dating counterparts?" Chance stalked to the edge of the stage and fake whispered into the mic, "And men who don't settle down see a reduction in penis length at the rate of three centimeters a year after forty if they haven't found a permanent partner?"

"None of that is true. He's making that up," Claire said while Hazel gave Lashes another stare. He didn't seem alarmed at the wild accusations Chance was slinging.

"Do those facts scare you? I hope you know they're false. As far as I know, anyway."

Claire leaned in and whispered, "See?" in Hazel's ear.

"That's what the media wants you to believe. They try to shame you into finding love. And here at Booty Camp, we want to tell you we're here for a great reason. It's okay to be single. It's okay to be satisfied with your life on your own. We just happen to know that that's not your feelings. No one pays a thousand dollars because they want to be alone."

Claire and Hazel looked at each other. Claire mouthed, "Well, *maybe you* do," which prompted Hazel to punch the top of her friend's arm.

"There is the desire to find a match, but at Booty Camp, we believe in destiny. That you are put on a path to lead you somewhere in particular."

Chance stooped lower and spoke to the first row like he was in a hair band in the 80s.

"Our competitors will say that if you have enough matching interests, you can get together and make a go of this crazy world. And that may be true, but here at Booty Camp, we want you to find The One. Your Happily Ever After.

The prince, or princess, of your dreams. We believe in one true love for every person. That's why we're better. You *will* find your other half. The apple to your peach. The butter on your toast. We seek perfection. And we find it."

Chance delivered the last lines straight to Claire. The whole room must have felt the chemistry between them because people turned and craned their necks to see who, exactly, had inspired that level of intensity from the speaker. Claire's lips were opened slightly, almost breathlessly. She reached for Hazel's hand and squeezed it like they were about to go down the scariest hill on a roller coaster together.

Claire looked so enchanted it was like she was acting in a movie.

She kept her eyes on the speaker, but spoke quietly to Hazel. "I'm going to marry that man."

Hazel's mouth dropped open.

Insta Love

"So you're in love now. Literally in love in the first 20 minutes of this shit show." Hazel crossed her arms and tapped her foot.

Claire was too busy watching Chance move around the theater.

Hazel and Claire had stood up after the presentation had come to a conclusion. Dark Lashes was nowhere to be found. Which was fine. Hazel had learned her painful lesson about looking for love in general. Scott was a great-looking guy, and he'd been a selfish, thoughtless user.

It had been three months since he walked out of her apartment with his beer. He'd been nailing the hyena upstairs every chance he got. It was demoralizing.

Hazel folded her hands together and let her thumbs wrestle each other. Being here was a stupid impulse and a waste of money. Not that she needed the money to move out because her landlord was strictly enforcing the two year agreement she's signed with him nine months ago.

Claire's body was pretty much humming when the very popular Chance made his way over to her.

"Ladies."

He was debonair. And looked like maybe he slept in a steroid hyperbolic chamber. He was body-builder ripped.

He'd said "*ladies*," but he was looking at Claire like she was a grilled chicken meal that fit right into his training program.

"Let me give you a moment. I need to run to the restroom." Hazel backed away from the get together, but she needn't have said anything to either of them. They were foolish for one another.

Hazel fluttered her fingertips at the very interested-looking guys herded together as she padded across the thick carpet on her tiptoes. She felt like she was on the green at a golf course. This had been such a horrific mistake. She wanted her money back. She couldn't trust a single man in the room. All she could manage was a mental image of each of them glaring at her while she naked-crouched after sex. Every man here was just a future Scott.

Hazel opened the closet door, hoping for the bathroom, but instead she got a peek at Dark Lashes sitting at a desk with easily a hundred Polaroids in front of him. He looked like he was concentrating. He was holding sets of pictures clipped together in what looked like pairs.

He whipped his head around just as she was trying to back out of the room.

"Can I help you?" Irritation oozed from every syllable.

Enough. Enough of his dismissive actions and his attitude. She was so fed up with men. Instead of telling him the truth—she'd picked the wrong door while looking for the bathroom—she put her hands on her hips and set her attitude free.

"Yes. I need my check back. I want out of this whole farce. Who do I see about that? The musclehead? Is he the owner of this pony show?" She did her best to stare him down.

Dark Lashes lifted his eyebrows. "You wrote a *check*?"

Okay, his voice was like KY Jelly for the air, making it slippery and ready for sex. His scrutiny made her tongue forget that it had requirements and a job.

Those damn blue eyes were making her hands sweat.

"Who writes checks anymore?" He turned his attention back to the desk and pictures. "Go find staff and mention it to them. I'm pretty sure checks are scanned and handled almost like credit cards. They'll help you. I have to concentrate."

Dismissed. Hazel felt her eyes narrowing. He was dismissing her. She was having flashbacks to the naked crouching, again. Scott had given her as little consideration as this man seemed to.

She battled her feistiness now. She wasn't naked. And she wasn't going to be dismissed.

"You know what?" Hazel stepped forward and slammed the door behind her, sealing Dark Lashes in with her. "Maybe a thousand dollars isn't a lot to you, but I'm a teacher, and this whole scam is pissing me off. My friend caught me at a weak moment after my ex-boyfriend humiliated me, otherwise I would've never agreed to do it. I want my money back. Now. A hundred and ten percent satisfied, my ass. You're wearing one of those horrible shirts. You're going to get up and get my money back or so help me..."

He set the pictures down on the surface of the desk and turned again. He looked her up and down. "Humiliated you?

And you put up with that?"

"Are you *judging* me? I didn't ask for your frigging opinion. I asked for my money."

Dark Lashes stood up, and Hazel worked to keep her heels cemented as he approached her.

She had been under the impression that he was short. At the least, no taller than she was, but she was wrong. He'd just looked small next to the Goliath who'd been transfixed by her best friend in the theater. Dark Lashes had at least six inches on her—even while she was wearing heels. He crossed his arms in front of him and got so close he could whisper and she'd be able to hear him.

His dark hair fell forward to cover one of his eyes, and she noticed the leather bracelets on the forearm with the tattoo. She tried to ignore his sharp jaw and defined cheekbones. He really was pretty. His attitude sucked donkey tits, though. And Hazel was sick of guys like him making her feel like she wasn't enough. She was getting her goddamned money back now. It was a pride thing.

"Hazel Lavender. Likes cats. Likes mountain biking and crafting. Looking for someone who will hold her hand at a scary movie and must love kids." He lifted just one eyebrow.

"Awesome. You read the ination my best friend sent in before we got here. Then you must be able to find my check pretty damn quick. I'll be needing it." Hazel snapped her fingers in an effort to get him to hurry up.

The door behind her opened without a knock. Turning at the waist, she saw it was Chance. And from the familiar leopard-print shoe she could see past him in the open doorway, she knew Claire was just outside.

"You ready, Wolf? We got a whole group of people out here." Chance gave Hazel a look that insinuated something very non-business worthy was going on at the moment.

"I'll be a minute." Dark Lashes—aka Wolf, apparently— nodded expectantly.

"You can take Claire Paquet out of the piles or pictures. FYI." Chance pointedly did not make eye contact beyond her and closed the door.

When Hazel turned around to look at her check's hostage-taker again, he was massaging his temples. Watching his fingers move wasn't the least bit arousing. Hazel shifted her weight from one foot to the other.

He shook his head and looked back at Hazel, again with the once-over. "Do you even know how many guys pulled me aside and pointed you out? And the number of notes that were passed from my staff with requests from the single guys in there?"

Hazel shook her head. Instead of feeling encouraged, she just pictured a bunch of Scotts in a line, waiting to break her heart.

"Ten. Ten of the guys in there are desperate to be your match. And they're just the ones who were forward enough to pass a word to us. I bet there's another ten praying to whatever they believe in that you're the one for them."

Hazel swallowed before responding to his obvious salesmanship. "Don't even with your As Seen On TV love stories. I made the mistake of coming here, but I want my money back."

"You afraid of love, Hazel?"

"Stop saying my name as if you know me. You don't know

me. It just makes you sound like an unscrupulous car salesman." Hazel tapped her foot so it would slap the wood floor with audible irritation.

He looked at her foot. "Oh, are you in a rush? I have to get back out there and I'm already behind, but you're the one who's unhappy?"

Hazel stepped up to him and pointed at his chest. "You. Them. This. A hundred and ten percent. Which is dumb because there's only one hundred percent of anything. Math. That's math. You can't just make up new math."

He closed one eye. "I haven't even had anything to drink, and your little rant is making me feel like I've been on a bender all night. Did that make sense to you?"

"Yes. Give me my money back. That's what I meant." She poked him in the chest. It was hard. She tried not to notice.

"Fine. You know what, *Hazel?*"

Hazel narrowed her eyes at him and stuck out her chest..

"I assume you read the fine print on the agreement you signed about an hour and a half ago. Right? You'd never sign a contract without looking it over properly."

He walked over to the desk again and ruffled through the pile of applications before pulling hers out so quickly she assumed the stack was alphabetized. "Hazel Lavender. Very neat signature. Fitting for a teacher. Can you tell me what it says there?"

He walked back to her and turned the paper around so it was facing her. He pointed to the bottom of the page at what looked a lot like fancy edging. When she squinted, she could see there were tiny words.

"Are you kidding me? Is this a joke? No one can even read

those words. I can't even imagine how illegal this is to do to people." Hazel pushed the paper back at him.

His motion to snatch it back filled the air with his light cologne because he was so close. *Jesus.* If her lady bits were a petting zoo, that scent would be what the zoo offered as a treat in the coin machine outside her cage.

She made eye contact as the attraction flared through her.

He held her gaze and bit his bottom lip before letting the tip of his tongue peek out briefly. Then he shook his head and went back to the matter at hand as if time had not just stopped for them both. "It's legal. It says that you're required to participate in five dates set up by Booty Camp experts before we have to refund your money."

"That's horse shit." Hazel shook her head.

"It's business. And if you need a bit of hope, no one has ever needed their money back. We're that good at our jobs. So, I think this is good news for you." He took her contract back to the desk and refiled it amongst the others.

Hazel felt trapped. And she didn't like it. That contract was a problem. She didn't want to be in some freaky, surefire love. The last time she was in love her heart had been ripped out of her chest.

"This was a huge mistake. I want my money now." She stalked over to the edge of the desk and tried to reach around him to get to her contract. She was planning on taking it and tearing it up.

He snatched her wrist and quickly twirled her. Before she knew it, her back was against his chest. He had both of her wrists and had managed to cross her arms over her chest. A restraint. And clearly not the first one he'd put someone in.

"Let go of me." Hazel got calmer.

"Only if you'll stay away from this business's personal property." He spoke the words into her hair, and she felt chills down her neck.

She looked at the hold he had her in. He may have restrained people, but her role as the special education teacher had required her to get restraint training, too. And she knew how to get out of this one. Because he wasn't a student, but a full-grown man with his hands on her, she added a little spice to her maneuver. She stomped on his foot and, at the same moment, used all her force to push her wrists against where his index fingers and thumbs were touching.

It worked. Once free, she turned and pushed hard on his chest, though that part he seemed ready for and stood strong. She wound up pushing against him so hard that she lost her balance and fell backwards. She landed hard on her bottom before she cracked her head on the hardwood floor.

Just before everything went completely fuzzy, she saw Claire looking at her from the doorway.

Y♡u Killed Her

Wolf knew Chance would try and hurt him now that the new love of his life was adjusting her friend's skirt to cover her light blue underwear. It looked bad; he understood that. But he hadn't touched her. Well, he'd restrained her when she was trying to get her contract back, but the rest was on her. She'd broken the hold and went all Rambo on his ass.

He felt awful when her head hit the floor. But before he could offer any aid, her red-headed friend was all over her, checking for a pulse and launching an incredible array of filthy curses at him.

Chance was out the door and back with an icepack for Hazel's head while Wolf stood there like a jackhole with his hands shoved in his pockets.

As Hazel was coming around, Claire went from a cursing, angry sailor to comforting friend in a hot minute. Chance shook his head as though Wolf had just kicked a puppy with another puppy on its back.

He mouthed to his friend, "*It wasn't my fault.*"

Chance mouthed back indigently, "*I know that.*"

At least Chance knew who he was. This was bad. Really

bad.

Wolfgang Shakespeare Saber ran Booty Camp Dating Service on the strict principle of making the customer happy. The happiest they had been in their entire lives, actually. Which would be a tough task for anyone else. But not for him. At least not where matchmaking was concerned.

Wolf's mother, grandmother, great-grandmother, and most likely beyond were matchmakers. Well, his mother and grandmother were still matchmakers in Boca Raton, Florida. They set up the lonesome in her retirement park all the time to great success. Being able to sense who would pair beautifully with whom was a gift that traveled through their family tree.

The women in his family provided the service from a place in their heart that cared about humanity. He'd been the first to monetize it. Which was strongly frowned upon, to put it lightly.

As he watched Claire help Hazel into a sitting position, he could almost feel his ancestors giving him an exasperated middle finger from the heavens above. And probably his mother and grandmother would do the same on FaceTime if he told them the truth of the situation. Which he wouldn't.

Hazel was forcing him to make mistakes. Before she had barged in here to demand her money back, he'd been facing the agonizing decision of who to place her with for her first date.

Wolf could sense energies that would work well together. It wasn't any paranormal bullshit, but his family had always been able to get a good read on people. The chemistry that made them who they were was highlighted for him and every woman in his family tree. He was the first male to be able to do the matchmaking, as far as they could tell.

All the other dating services matched up questionnaires and used math and statistics to place together people who sought a mate.

Not Booty Camp.

Wolf had his staff take a Polaroid of the clients. It didn't have to be a Polaroid—it could be any picture, but he liked the feel of the Polaroid for matching energies. And then he would make piles of like energies. Some went together like salt and pepper or bread and butter—but that was rare. Usually in a group, there would be a few energies that would work together.

Hence the dating portion of the business. If the pheromones and life experiences were a miss, the couple would be less inclined to meet up with each other. Any leftovers from the city before—there was always one or two, but never more than five—would be matched with someone in the next city.

A hundred and ten percent correct. He would find someone for everyone. Having the business was genius. It brought people with open energies together and made his matchmaking job so much easier. For two years he'd been matching the hell out of people. His staff were not allowed to date clients, but they'd seen how every single person was eventually matched, so they believed wholeheartedly in what they were doing.

Before he was puzzling over Hazel's matches, he'd checked out Chance's and Claire's energies. They were an off-the-charts match. Chance's cheesy photo in the flier was a singsong match for Claire's vibrant Polaroid. Wolf had been pissed that Chance had made so many obvious passes at the woman, but after seeing the pictures, he knew this was the very match his friend needed in his life.

And Wolf had made a horrible first impression by having the woman's friend sprawled out on the floor, skirt above her waist, when Claire walked in.

He sighed. "Can I get you a glass of water? An aspirin? Do we need an ambulance?"

It hadn't been that hard a knock on the head, but the skull was a crazy place and Hazel could be more injured than he thought.

"Or the cops?!" Claire put her arm around her friend's shoulders.

Hazel put her hand on Claire's arm. "He wasn't trying to hurt me. Stop me from taking back my illegal contract, yes, but I fell off balance. I still hate him. And I still want my money back."

Wolf squatted low and put out a hand. "I'm truly sorry. I wasn't expecting you to attack. And the only reason I put up any resistance is I've been looking at the matches and you have so many that are close to a perfect selection. I think you need to stay. For your future."

Claire spoke before Hazel could. "Of course you want her to stay. Look at her. Jesus, her rack is the thing of dreams, and her face looks like the result of a Victoria Secret model having sex with Aphrodite's brother. Her skin is perfect, and her ass is the best I've ever seen in jeans."

Hazel looked at her knees, blushing.

Claire was right. Wolf had been all over the country in

rooms full of single women for years now, and he'd never had his mouth go dry at the sight of any of them. He'd even tripped a little when he saw Hazel.

Her brown hair was long and shiny, and her big blue eyes could probably start a few wars. There was no ignoring her body, with its tiny waist and ass that could make grown men cry. Hazel was more than that, though, the way her face was so inviting. She was exactly what his soul pictured when it heard the word lovely.

"Men are usually willing to hump a cactus to get her number. So I'm not surprised. But your manhandling her goes through me." Claire helped Hazel to her feet.

Chance gave him bug eyes.

Wolf tossed up his hands and mouthed, "*Fix this.*"

Wolf's best friend was on his team for a reason: Chance was great at people. If peopleing was a definable skill, Chance would have a Masters in it. Wolf often led people to believe that Chance was the owner of Booty Camp because, while Wolf could help people become happy, he was far too gruff to deal with the public.

"Beautiful Claire, please. Understand my buddy here would never hurt any woman on purpose. Honestly. He's been known to go to the venue a couple was going to for a date for the first time just to make sure it went well. He's really caring, he just has the social skills of a hiney badger." Chance bit his lip then went about correcting himself, "Honey badger. Sorry. Hiney badgers would be bad."

Wolf put his palm to his forehead. His go-to guy was fumbling. It figured. Chance was probably off his rocker because he was so close to Claire.

Hazel held out her hand. "The check. That's all I want."

Wolf cringed. "I'm sorry, checks get automatically deposited, and there's a whole process that will take at least two weeks, maybe more. If you had paid with a credit card, this would have been a simple refund."

Hazel shook her head and touched her temple.

"You okay?" Chance asked.

"No. I think I feel a lawsuit coming on." Hazel looked straight at him with her big blue eyes.

Chance chuckled. "She's got all those guys out there with their hearts in their hands *and* a sense of humor. Too bad you can't have more than one husband at a time in this state."

Wolf gave Chance a look that he hope conveyed: *Please, for the love of everything holy, please stop talking.*

Chance missed the look because he was too busy staring at Claire.

Hazel rolled her eyes and turned her back on him. Claire followed her out but not before touching Chance's hand.

Chance shut the door behind them and took a second to gather his thoughts. "What's the deal? Just give her cash back? Also, Claire's my match, right? I mean, she has to be."

Wolf walked back to his chair and collapsed. He picked up the picture of Hazel between his index finger and middle finger like it was a baseball card he might throw.

"Claire's your match. Best one I've ever seen. You can't date her until we are out of town, though." Wolf looked at Hazel in the picture, her eyes were wary. She was hurting. Her energy was extremely fragile.

So many of the men on the table would be a great match

for her. The caretaking energy was strong with at least three of them. Not soul mate matches, but stable guys.

But Wolf felt something he'd never encountered before when making a match.

He felt jealous.

Wolf Is Not Even
A Normal Name

Hazel leaned against the wall outside the office while Claire fussed over her.

"Are you sure you're okay? I will go back in there and show him what it feels like to have a redhead rip out your nut hair."

Hazel smiled. "No, I'm fine. I barely hit my head, really. I've knocked my head harder on my kitchen cabinets. But I *would* like to see that whole attack go down."

Claire fixed Hazel's hair. "I just got this manicure, so maybe as soon as I get my first chip in it, I'll come back and have at him."

"Is his name Wolf? Is that what I heard?" Hazel picked up a pamphlet from the side table that had been pushed against the wall. The staff was listed at the bottom of the last page. Sure enough *Wolfgang Shakespeare Saber* was listed as one of the last employees. "Yup. There he is. I guess we know exactly what you name a pretentious asshole."

"In my mother's defense, she didn't know I would turn out this way." Wolf had exited the office just in time to hear Hazel's comment.

Hazel narrowed her eyes at the man holding a thick file. "Maybe she was a baby-naming savant. Because she nailed it."

Wolf gave her a sideways smirk. Chance touched Claire's shoulder and smiled. "Come on, this is the best part. We set up the first dates. They'll happen in a minute."

Claire checked with Hazel, and she gave the universal gesture for okay to show her friend that she'd be all right.

She overheard Chance whisper to Claire, "Is it okay if they don't set you up? I just can't imagine letting any other man take you on a date."

Her friend batted her eyelashes before answering like Marilyn Monroe singing Happy Birthday. "Oh yes. I think that would be amazing. Plus, you didn't even take my money. So I can't partake."

Hazel lagged behind the star-struck lovebirds until Chance kissed Claire's cheek and bounded up to Wolf to snag the folder. As she looked around, she was pretty sure the staff was more excited than the clients, and that was saying something.

Chance revealed the names of the dating pairs as though they had won the *Price is Right* "Showdown Showcase."

And as Hazel watched skeptically from the back of the theater, single after single paired up. And they were acting like lovesick fools—well, most of them. The men were going overboard with the praise, and the ladies were eating it up the way they never would in a bar. Cheesy seemed to be the flavor of choice.

After the first wave of matches was made, the secondary matches were announced. Chance did a great job of explaining these were the matches that Booty Camp might require a bit of experimentation to get right. Hazel noticed neither her nor Claire's name had been mentioned.

Wolf approached them. "You still a confrontational jerk?"

Hazel shook her head while giving him the finger.

"Good, glad to see you're feeling like yourself."

Claire growled in Wolf's direction.

The Booty Camp staff began mingling through the crowd with appetizers, glasses of wine, and mugs of beer.

Chance came back to Claire and Hazel, leaving Wolf standing a little off to the side.

Chance looked legitimately concerned, checking on Hazel and asking her to close her eyes and open them as he shone the flashlight app on his phone into them.

"Equal and reactive. Do you have a headache at all? Are you feeling nauseous?"

Wolf toed the floor in what seemed to be embarrassment.

"Yes, I'm sick to my stomach that this guy stole my money, and because I paid with a check, I effectively have to hook myself out for five dates to earn my money back." Hazel widened her eyes in Wolf's direction.

Chance was a smooth talker, though, immediately launching into a convincing speech about how she could— nay, *would*—find a life partner and that in this world, having someone that understood her on a fundamental level would be beneficial and worth more than the admission fee. And getting the opportunity to be granted happiness was a chance millions were desperate to participate in. Chance got her to smile twice and laugh once.

When she finally shrugged, he launched into action,

putting his giant arm gently around her shoulders and leading her to the front of the room where two dudes were chatting with each other while glancing around the room. They were nice-looking. And when they saw Chance headed toward them with Hazel in tow, their faces lit up like Christmas morning.

Either of these guys would look great walking her to her apartment. Scott would have to walk past her and one of these suitors to get to the elevator. She would make sure of it.

When she was close enough to see that both men had brown eyes, Chance stopped in his tracks. Wolf began angrily whispering in his ear.

Hazel watched as a little of the sincere charm dropped from Chance's face, and his eyebrows knit together. He added loud enough for Hazel to hear, "Okay. You're the boss."

He turned to her and gave her an expectant smile. "Actually, those guys aren't your match. Um... your match wasn't able to make it tonight."

He steered her back to Claire, and Wolf made himself scarce after obviously sabotaging her future dates.

"So who is it, then? If it is not one of those guys."

Chance excused himself with a self-appointed job instead of answering her question. "You know what? You guys haven't gotten any of the hors d'oeuvres. Let me go grab some for us before they're all gone."

Claire stepped closer to Hazel. "Seriously, what was that about? I thought those guys were excited to see you?"

Wolf appeared with a glass of red wine for each of them.

"They were excited to see Chance, not Hazel. Look."

Hazel accepted the glass just as Claire did, and together they turned their heads in time to watch the two potential suitors hold hands.

Wolf cleared his throat. "They're a match for each other. We're two men shy tonight, so we'll have to wait to find your match." He indicated to Hazel with the knuckle of his index finger. "We'll send out a second wave of applications to replace those that got a match tonight."

"Are you kidding? You did this on purpose to keep my money. I am *not* a hundred and ten percent satisfied. I want to be a thousand dollars' worth of satisfied tonight!" As she finished, Hazel realized the entire theater had quieted.

Wolf lifted an eyebrow. "You're a tough lady to satisfy. We might need a car battery and jackhammer, so I hear."

Hazel felt the embarrassment crawl up her face as she realized what their argument sounded like. He was insinuating that she wanted someone to "service" her in the very oldest sense of the word.

Chance appeared with two more wine glasses, and Hazel narrowed her eyes.

"Oh, okay. I guess I'll get my thousand dollars' worth somehow." She chugged her wine and handed the empty to Claire. Then she took the two wine glasses from the tray Chance was holding and alternated taking slugs from each glass.

The conversation picked up again—quietly at first while Chance, Wolf, and Claire watched Hazel pound the alcohol.

God bless Claire, she was at least a good wingwoman, letting Hazel revenge drink.

When those two glasses were finally empty, Hazel shoved them at Wolf. "Here."

But it wasn't enough. Tops, she had ingested fifteen dollars' worth of wine. She looked around and spotted a very lush, expensive, framed picture on the wall.

Hazel went Scarlett O'Hara on the moment and walked up to it. "I bet this will fetch a price."

Hazel lifted the heavy picture off the wall and staggered a little under the weight of it. As soon as she had the picture balanced—which was quite a feat with heels on—she lifted her chin and addressed Wolf. "Good day, sir."

Chance put the tray under his arm and stepped forward, probably to relieve Hazel of the picture, but Wolf held up his hand, stopping him. "No, it's fine. We're renting the space and everything, but it's fine."

Hazel's dignity was now reliant on her staggering out of the fancy theater while holding onto a huge framed painting.

She managed to get to the first door when she remembered it wasn't automatic. Which was an issue. Wolf gallantly bowed and added some flourish with his hand before holding the door open for her.

"By all means, let me help you commit this bold misdemeanor."

Hazel was really reconsidering her brazen problem-solving as she shouted to Claire, "Are you cool if I leave? This is heavy."

Claire gave her a very confused-looking thumbs up, but Hazel wrangled the painting out the door. Wolf trailed behind only to sprint ahead and hold the second door for her.

When she was on the sidewalk, she realized she had to set it down to use her car service app. She executed a very unfeminine squat to place her new painting on the ground and let the top rest against her hip while she dug around for her phone.

Wolf stood nearby, arms folded, watching her.

"What?" She called up a car and received the confirmation that it was about three minutes away.

"You're going to keep going with this?" He gestured to the giant painting.

"Yes." She gripped the frame again now that her phone was tucked away.

"How are you going to get it in the car?" He closed one eye while he appeared to size up the giant piece of artwork.

"With my arms. And my anger. It'll work." The wine that she'd pounded was hitting her pretty hard. That was the last thing she needed him to see. "Why are you standing here?"

"It's been a while since I had a video go viral online, so I think you jamming that painting you stole into a stranger's car while all dressed up might be the fuel my social media presence needs right now." He held up his phone and said, "Smile."

She held up her middle finger to the ass-clencher for the third time in the last hour.

The car service pulled up, and the woman who got out to greet her was already shaking her head.

"Yeah, I hope you're leaving that with your boyfriend because there's no way that will fit in here."

"He's not my boyfriend." She gave Wolf a dirty look.

"I like to refer to myself as the latest victim of her most

recent crime spree." He pretended to shine his ring on his T-shirt.

"Okay. Who am I taking where?" The driver obviously had a busy night ahead of her.

Hazel felt unexpected tears trying to make an ass out of her. She bit her tongue.

Wolf stepped forward and opened his wallet. "How much can I pay you for coming here to witness this?"

Hazel held on to the painting while Wolf settled up the bill.

"She and I will sort this issue out, and we can try to call you again. Thanks for your patience." He accepted the business card from the driver before she left.

"How's your head?" It was chilly outside. And her top was dangerously close to revealing even more about her than she wanted Wolf finding out.

"It's great. I'm great." Hazel felt like the heels on her shoes might be uneven.

He stepped forward and held her elbow.

"Can we bring the picture back inside the theater? Because I'm not a critic, but I think the frame alone is worth more than I owe you." He lifted it easily.

The fight was draining out of her, anyway. This whole night was a disaster. It was like the naked crouching in front of Scott while he broke up with her was the start of a horrible horror novel. And this was the next chapter. Maybe everything she touched from now on would be a pile of crap.

"Can you get the door or are you just going to stand there and pout?"

Wolf gestured with his foot.

"You know what? Screw you. No. I'm not opening the door.

You can go screw yourself. I'm done being humiliated by your gender. You can stick that painting up your ass."

Hazel put her hands on her bare shoulders and started walking home. She had to look down to try and pick out a straight line.

Right now would be a great time to throw up. It would probably be the healthiest thing. However, one of Hazel's skills was never tossing her cookies. Strong stomach or whatever. She was a glass-and-a-half kind of girl. Pounding three glasses in less than fifteen minutes was going to make her feel like she was getting tea-bagged by an angry clown in the morning. Getting home while she froze her tits off was great as well. Maybe while trying to retain heat, her body would burn off the alcohol and she'd sober up.

She stumbled again and contemplated her footwear. She didn't want to walk barefoot on the sidewalk in the city.

Hazel sighed. She'd maybe made it two blocks when she had to give up and die. Her feet turned inward in an effort to keep her up—like she was snowplowing down a bunny hill.

And then he was behind her, holding her hips. "Whoa there, Capone. You all right?"

She elbowed him in the stomach, but not too hard. She was a tiny huge bit blasted, and it was getting worse, but she didn't want him to sue her any more than she wanted to sue him. Court sucked.

"Capone?" His nickname registered after the weak scuffle. "He was a criminal, too."

She tried to slap his face over her shoulder and missed. She did, however, succeed in throwing herself off balance.

He ducked and caught her, lifting her into his arms before

she could fall.

"Damn, girl. What the hell?"

Hazel felt like her lips might be numb. "Why are all the pretty boys assholes?"

"Are you saying I'm pretty?" He was walking with her now. Her cheek was bouncing off his shoulder.

"I'm saying you're an asshole." She grabbed a fistful of his shirt.

"You're freezing." He pulled her closer as he carried her in the direction of the theater.

There was a distinct breeze in her chest area. "Don't look at my tits."

"You ask things that aren't even human."

He set her on her feet on the teeny stairs in front of the theater and covered his eyes with one hand, holding her shoulder with the other, while she pulled up Claire's tiny top.

"All good?" He spread his fingers so he could look at her face through the gaps.

She turned to walk in the theater because the cold had superseded her pride and she needed to warm up.

He had to steady her again as the tiny steps demanded better gross motor skills than she had at the moment.

"Just give me a second."

She faced him with what she hoped was an aggravated glare as he put a hand on her hip, peeled off his Booty Camp T-shirt, and shook it out with his free hand.

His chest was mesmerizing. He was the perfect kind of lean-chiseled that told anyone checking him out that he could easily carry a woman two blocks but not enough muscle to make a person wonder if his balls had shrunk up

DEBRA ANASTASIA

like two jingle bells. And the tattoos.

The colorful tattoos were artwork that included shading and highlighting and elegantly lettered foreign words.

"They should put that heavy frame around these dazzling nipples." Hazel wanted to chew on one of the tannish-pink erogenous zones. Then she looked in his eyes. They reflected surprise and a little amusement. At least that's what her wine-soaked brain perceived.

He let go of her hips to pop his T-shirt over her head. She watched his hands for a few seconds before she cooperated and threaded her arms through the holes.

It was still slightly warm from his body, and she let out a happy—yet accidental—moan.

Chance opened the door for them from the inside. Claire was there, looking concerned.

"Hey, can you hang that picture back up? And check it for damage?" Wolf put his arm around her waist and led her back to his office.

Claire came to her side. "Are you hurt?"

Hazel wanted to shake her head but wound up just using her eyeballs to make the motion.

Claire touched her cheek while keeping up with Wolf's pace for her.

"Holy crap. You're straight fucked up."

Hazel wrinkled her nose in agreement.

Wolf pulled her through the door and helped her to the chair in front of the desk where he'd been looking at pictures when she first came to fight for her money.

Chance popped his head back in. "Picture is back in its rightful spot and looks perfectly intact. So we're good."

42

Hazel wanted to give Wolf an "I told you so" facial gesture, but she caught her reflection in the mirror behind the desk and saw that she was replicating the "Wiley E. Coyote getting slapped in the face with a frying pan" expression instead. She replaced it quickly with a frown and looked at her lap.

Chance spoke up again, "Listen, I'm about to coach the group share. Can I take Claire for that? I want her to see it in action."

Claire was petting the top of Hazel's head, which made her wonder how much her best friend had been drinking, as well.

"Is that okay? Can I leave you here with Wolf?"

"*Wolf* is such a dumb name." Hazel flipped her hair and got it stuck in what was left of her lip gloss. Pulling it free became an all-consuming task.

"She's fine here. I'll make sure she has a bucket if she hurls." Wolf gave Chance a quick thumbs-up.

Hazel watched as Wolf pulled a button-up shirt over his bare chest. She was sad to see the nipples go as he fastened it closed.

"What's the group share?" Hazel poked the word Booty Camp on the front of his T-shirt she was wearing.

"You want your money back. You don't get our secrets." He sat down on the other side of the desk and started sifting through some paperwork.

"Don't you have to go?" Maybe she should just be quiet until she was more sober. She scratched at her scalp to try to hurry the process.

He regarded her again but didn't answer before getting up without a word and walking out.

"Dick," Hazel muttered. He didn't even have the decency to answer a question.

She heard the crowd of people outside laughing together. Now she was even more curious about the group share.

Wolf walked back in and set a pile of crackers on her side of the desk. "Let's try and dilute that alcohol a little." He cracked open an ice-cold water bottle and handed it to her. Then he dragged the waste paper basket close to her feet and gestured to it. "In case eating makes you more... productive. And no, I don't have to go to the group share. My job is done for now." He sat back down and rustled through the papers again.

"So you're just the mean one? Is that what you do? I'm surprised Chance lets you work for him." Hazel crossed her legs, and one of her high heels fell off. She pretended it didn't happen.

Wolf looked from her face to her foot and back again. "You just going to leave that there?"

"I wanted to take it off." She gave him her best poker face.

"Chance works for me, not the other way around." He pulled out his phone and appeared to use it as a calculator.

"So you mean you're his boss? Man, you must be related to somebody. You have no people skills." She ruffled her hair.

He gave her an exasperated eye roll. "I own this. Booty Camp. The whole company. It's mine."

She squinted at him. "What. What? You own this whole nightmare?"

He didn't answer but gave her a dark look.

"Oh, that explains the stupid name." She pointed at the name on the shirt again. She could feel the light bulb of an idea forming. "So, really, you're the one who owes me my thousand dollars directly." She uncrossed her legs and put her hands on her lap. "Pay up."

He clucked his tongue at her. "Oh no. That went into the business account. I can't touch those funds until the banks have cleared the transfers. I don't dip into personal money when it comes to Booty Camp. It'd be a huge tax hassle."

She stood up. And remembered her shoe was off, so she was lopsided.

He stood up as well. "And I'm not sure if you're done trying to vandalize the place I've rented for this leg of the Booty Camp tour."

"Did you design the tacky butt as a heart emblem yourself too?" She put her hands on her hips.

"We prefer to call it cute. And inviting." He crossed his arms over his chest. His blue eyes were sparkling a little. Like he was enjoying sparring with her. Like it was unusual to have someone do so.

"Inviting you to donate a thousand dollars to the Booty cause, no doubt." She placed one hand on the desk near the crackers and tried to nonchalantly put her other damn shoe on.

"People get their money's worth around here. You'd be our first failure, love." He lifted one eyebrow.

She looked down at her feet as she put on her shoe and hoped she'd broken the eye contact before he saw how much his words had hurt her.

It was all too soon. She wasn't done hurting over Scott yet. She wasn't done hearing him bring another woman to orgasm over her head every night. All of this was too soon.

She sat back down.

"I'm kidding. I mean, you would be the first failure, but I'm sure you're much more pleasant when you're sober and not stealing things. There has to be someone out there for you."

She heard him walking around the desk. Then she could see his big boots next to the tips of her shoes.

Hazel said nothing.

"Maybe drink your water."

She got that he was probably trying to be helpful—in his gruff way—but it was harsh to her ears.

She reached past his hip and snagged the bottle. She took a few sips.

Music started playing in the theater.

"What's that?"

"The mandatory slow dance." He cleared his throat and reshuffled his folded arms.

She hazarded a look at his face. He'd be almost as pretty as a lady. If he didn't have the Adam's apple and muscular forearms.

"You literally recreate everyone's middle school dream here, huh?" Hazel took another drink.

He ran a hand over his mouth before offering, "Humans are pretty basic. What we wanted when we started puberty is pretty much what we want now. To be accepted. To fit in and be asked to dance or have your partner say yes. Simple stuff. With the right person, the romantic stuff isn't cheesy anymore."

"How does your girlfriend feel about your job?"

He bit the insides of his cheeks for a second, highlighting his high cheekbones. Seriously, blush would work on his face.

"No girlfriend. One ex-wife." He ran his hand through his dark hair.

She was sure her eyebrows said, *"Wow."* She slouched down in her chair and tried to keep the criticism from her expression.

"Happy now?" He pushed away from the desk and turned his back to her.

"I'm just thinking maybe I'm not destined to be Booty Camp's first failure. Maybe that statistic is already on the books." Hazel shrugged.

"Fair point. You're right. I'm the owner and the first failure." He sat in his chair.

Hazel leaned forward and held her temples while she put her elbows on her knees.

Chance knocked briefly on the partly open door before stepping in. "All good. We've got the A's set up and locked into date two, and now the B's are mingling."

Wolf looked at her while he suggested, "How about two more slow songs? Lower the lights and send out another tray of drinks. And make sure we have plenty of cabs out front. No drunk drivers or ladies who can't make it home."

Chance stood around for a beat, obviously wanting to ask something else.

Wolf finally looked away from her and at the action-hero shaped man in the doorway.

"Um. Any chance I can nip out early? I'd really like to take Claire somewhere more private." Claire inched past Chance to Hazel's side.

Hazel looked at Wolf and mentioned, "I thought there was

no dating clients?"

She realized her mistake when she saw the betrayal on Claire's face. She whispered, "I'm sorry."

"Well, Capone, because your friend lives in the twenty-first century and paid with a credit card, we'll be able to reverse her charges so she's not considered a client. So I'll allow it." He drummed his long fingers on the desk blotter. "It's normally frowned upon, but for Chance I'm willing to bend the rules."

Chance cleared his throat, "I actually comped her, Wolf."

Wolf nodded as if this information wasn't a breech of company policy.

There was just something in Hazel's chemistry that made her want to fight with Wolf more than anything else, so she found herself speaking up, "No. You don't get to decide the fate of my best friend like a sweeping dictator with your middle school dances and your expensive self-made brothel. How do I even know that he"—she pointed at Chance—"isn't some sort of murdering weirdo on the side? I came here with Claire; she goes home with me. Girlfriends don't leave each other behind. It's the best friend code."

Hazel sat up straighter even though it made her head spin a little. Claire tapped her shoulder and began whispering in Hazel's ear.

"When we were slow dancing, I felt his dong and it's like a fist, I want to ride it like it's the last train to heaven."

Hazel watched Wolf fail to cover his grin with his hand.

"Damn it."

Claire hugged Hazel from behind and fluffed her hair for her as a parting favor.

"Can I go with him? Please? They all have to get background checks and stuff. Wolf runs this place like it's a branch of the FBI. Speaking of things like branches." Claire pointed at Chance's crotch with her pinkie in a way that was not nearly as discreet as she thought it was.

"How am I getting home?" She turned to look at her friend.

Claire fixed Hazel's hair again while she gave her the plan. "Chance promised me Wolf would see you home. And he can't kill you or anything because that would be bad for business."

"*Really*? This is happening?" Hazel grabbed Claire's hand.

"It's like a salami and a beer can had a baby." Claire gave Hazel the pleading eyes.

"I swear if this man kills me tonight, I'll haunt you and all of your descendants forever." Hazel pulled on Claire so her friend fell onto her lap, and they hugged.

"I know." Claire lightly pinched Hazel's cheeks to add some color and asked, "Did you blow chunks?" Hazel shook her head. "I swear you have the strongest stomach. You could handle a bucket of cum from an alligator." Claire kissed the top of Hazel's head, and Hazel's stomach rolled at her friend's description.

Then Claire got up and left with Chance like he was the Pied Piper of Penis and Hazel was left to be escorted home by the man who had essentially stolen her money.

Getting Her H♡me

Wolf watched Chance and Claire leave. He had a big night ahead of him. There was a lot of accounting to do, making sure the space was left clean, and starting to work on the second string of Booty Camp applicants.

But his unhappy customer needed to get home. The fact that she was still pretty drunk was an issue. And she was wearing his shirt. Which came all the way past her skirt, so it looked like that was all she was wearing with her heels, and he hated how much he liked that idea.

Hazel was stunning. But she acted like she had no clue her face and body were a punch right in the junk. She almost seemed like someone had stolen her self-confidence.

It would be easier to get her home now and then stay late. He had enough staff to keep this well-running machine going for another hour.

Booty Camp's tour of America had been legendary in dating circles. And Wolf's mother and grandmother wildly disapproved. They said he was going against the energy he'd been blessed with by being able to sense who belonged with who in this crazy world.

They blamed his divorce on his exploitation of the gifts their family had been given.

And that had hurt. Honestly. That was the kicker, though. The matchmaker couldn't find a match for himself. His grandmother had told him from the beginning of his relationship with Clarisse that they were off. Close, she'd said, but off.

He was pigheaded, and he'd married her anyway. When Clarisse left him, it was for her very own perfect match she'd met at a Booty Camp event. She'd dropped by to see him at work and had broken up with him before the night was over.

And he hadn't stopped her because he'd seen the energies were a gorgeous match.

That was the rub, according to his mother and grandmother. There was never a match for a matchmaker. Nothing permanent, anyway.

Wolf double-checked that his cell phone had a charge before waving over Vin.

"I have to take this one home. She's had too much to drink. You're in charge until I'm back. Okay?"

Vin looked pleased beyond reason and stood up straighter. Chance was always second in command, but Vin was hungry for more advancement in the company. Peter, the head of security, was absent and Vin had picked up extra jobs that had opened up.

Wolf stepped closer to Hazel and told Vin to call them the car from earlier.

"So you don't have a jacket at all?" He held out his hand to her to help her stand.

She stuck her tongue out at him.

It was pretty, just like her mouth. Full, kissable lips and bright white teeth made the gesture almost obscene.

He reached for his jacket from the coatrack in the office he was calling home base while in Garville and helped her into it after she stood.

"Don't pretend to be nice to me." She fluffed her hair out from under the collar.

"I won't. Don't worry. I'm keeping a close eye on you, sticky Capone. Let's get this whole situation on the road." Wolf stood next to her, but when she pulled her arm away from him twice, he let her manage her own balance.

She did okay. Outside was the same car service driver, but this time she approved of the lack of nineteenth-century art and opened the back door for them.

He closed the door behind Hazel and walked to the other side with the driver.

"She's okay?"

"Yeah. She's less angry now. I just want to get her home so she can sleep it off."

When Wolf slid in beside her, she was already holding up her middle finger.

"Delightful. Your charm is really overwhelming."

"Pyramid scam artist." Hazel leaned forward and spoke to the driver. "Have you ever been victim of a scam? This guy stole a thousand dollars from me tonight. And now I have to go on five dates to get my money back. Does that seem fair to you? Just because I paid for this stupid dating service with a check."

She sat back and folded her arms over the Booty Camp T-shirt and jacket.

"I always pay with checks. You get hacked too often with credit cards." The driver looked in the rearview window.

"Thank you!" Hazel glowered at him.

He felt compelled to defend himself. "It's not my policy, it's the bank's. I'm just saying if you manage to go on the dates before the check clears, then you can get your money back sooner."

Hazel ignored him and offered the next argument to the driver, who was apparently now judge and jury for the whole issue. "How shady does that sound?"

"Super shady." The driver agreed.

"Men." Hazel looked out the window. "You can't trust them. I swear. Now I'm headed home to listen to my ex-boyfriend drill his new girlfriend in his apartment right above mine for the rest of the evening."

"No!" The driver frowned.

"Oh yes. He cheated on me with her, and now I can't get out of my lease,"—Hazel shot Wolf a look—"which seems to be the theme of my life right now."

The driver sighed. "Sometimes life shits on us for a while. It could be worse."

Wolf looked out his window and felt a spark of sympathy for Hazel. He knew what being betrayed felt like, that was for sure.

"He's just such a dick about it. I mean, the new girlfriend lives in my building, too, so they could spend the night at her place where I wouldn't have to hear it. But no, they go to his place." Hazel ran her finger along the window. "And the girlfriend? She's so proud of herself for taking him from me. I swear she times things so I run into them constantly at the elevator or when I'm getting the mail."

Wolf cleared his throat. It explained why her energy was so tough to read. It was broken. The car pulled to the curb, and the driver turned and held out her hand to Hazel. "It'll be okay, sister. Hang in there."

Hazel smiled and thanked her, squeezing her hand in feminine camaraderie.

"Here, keep my card. I'll drive you where you need to go in the city."

Hazel opened her own door before saying, "Of course this stealer, stealer, pumpkin peeler will pay this fare."

"Of course," the driver replied.

Wolf frowned. The women were working against him.

He tapped the seat in front of him lightly. "Can you stay here? I want to make sure she gets into her place, and then I have to go back to the theater."

"Sure thing, sugar buns." The driver slid the car into Park and slapped on her four ways. "I'll give you ten minutes, then I'll roll out. You can call me if it takes longer, and I'll roll back and get you if I'm available."

Wolf opened the door after making sure the traffic had slowed.

Hazel was resting against the wall, obviously waiting for the elevator. He walked to the door, but it was locked.

Wolf decided that he would watch her get on the elevator since she was not making any attempt to come open the door for him. And then a couple came up behind him.

"There's your ex! Holy crap, she looks wasted. How sad. Can you feel me up in front of her again? I love to watch her change colors. She goes all green."

The man, who looked like a Ken doll come to life, pulled out a key card and tapped it on the device to open the door.

"Sure thing, baby. I love your mean streak."

As they entered the building, Wolf watched as Hazel's eyes found the loud couple.

They were fawning all over each other.

The defeat in Hazel's posture made Wolf grab the door before it closed and locked him out.

Her eyes looked moist before she aimed her gaze toward the floor. The two idiots were playacting their parts to make her extra miserable.

Wolf planned on regretting later what he was going to do now. She might even have him arrested for it, but he pushed the Ken doll out of the way like he was dying of thirst and Hazel was a glass of water.

She was surprised when she looked up to see him stalking her. She looked over her shoulder, saw only the wall, and turned back to him.

Wolf snaked one arm around her waist and slid his other arm behind her neck. Her grabbed a fistful of her brown hair and used it to guide her mouth to his.

He kissed the living hell out of her.

At first she was tense and unmoving. But he refused to let it stop him. The elevator's bell sounded as the doors opened.

When Ken doll and mean slut tried to step on to it, Wolf held out his arm out to block them.

He hefted Hazel, and she took the hint, hopping up and straddling him, koala style. He never stopped kissing her. Well, now she was kissing him while he used his arm to bar the others from the elevator.

The mean slut muttered, "That's some damn kiss."

Wolf turned and put Hazel against the wall. And he knew he was doing it for her, but everything she was doing in rebuttal was very welcome to his now rock-hard dick.

The doors closed behind them and the elevator started its assent before he forced himself to put her down.

She straightened his Booty Camp shirt and jacket on her body and covered her mouth with one hand. Then she slapped his chest with the other.

"What the hell was that?"

Wolf turned to try and avoid showing her everything he had to offer in his pants. The elevator was headed up, but he hadn't pushed a button. "What floor are you on?"

"What?" Hazel sounded breathless.

"Your floor number? So I can make sure you get home." Wolf kept his back to her as the elevator zoomed up to the eighth floor.

"I'm on the third. Why did you kiss me like you just came back from war?" Hazel touched his shoulder.

At least she wasn't slapping him anymore.

He pressed Three.

A person got on with a laundry basket, and the doors closed. Wolf waited until the elevator stopped again and held open the door for her but didn't follow her out.

She stepped onto the hall carpet and put her hand next to his, not letting the doors close. "Tell me why you kissed me."

He shrugged. "I didn't like the way you looked at your feet when they came into the lobby."

She stepped back. "A pity kiss? How much does that cost me?"

Wolf tossed up his hands. He'd been trying to be nice. The doors closed but not before he got a glimpse of her looking as broken as she had before he'd kissed her.

He rubbed his temple.

"You're pretty."

"Excuse me?"

The man holding the laundry basket repeated himself. "You're pretty."

"Thanks?" Wolf finally paid attention to the bizarre fact that this old man was doing his laundry at midnight.

"That's your answer. If she ever asks you that question again. The answer is always 'because you're pretty' or 'because I had to.' 'Because I can't breathe unless my skin is touching yours.' Any of those." The old man adjusted his grip on the basket.

"And you're the expert?" Wolf doubted that a man cleaning his undies on a Friday night could give him, the owner of Booty Camp, any advice.

"I was married for fifty-four years. You kiss a woman because she's beautiful to you. Any other reason and you don't deserve her lips." The elevator pinged its arrival at the lobby.

"*Was* married?"

"My Ethel passed last year." The man stepped into the lobby where Ken and mean slut were still waiting.

"Thanks for that advice." Wolf knew the guy was right. Fifty-four years of experience surely had him beat.

Ken Doll and slut started making out—maybe as retaliation—but Wolf looked at his phone to check the time, and he made it outside just as the car was pulling away. He

57

tapped the side and the driver stopped, popping the locks to let him inside. He'd just made a huge mistake. No kissing clients was his rule. And he broke it. He would have to convince Hazel to keep their lip-lock private as soon as possible. A lapse in judgment. But damn if everything about her wasn't soft and tempting and downright lovely.

S♥ He Kissed Her

Hazel looked at her reflection in the shiny metal of the elevator door. She touched her lips and her hair at the same time. Wolf could kiss. His lips actually tasted delicious. Like, not like a food, but in a way that totally worked for her lady parts.

And getting kissed like *that* in front of Scott and Hyena was probably worth a thousand dollars, if she was being honest.

She slid her heels off and picked them up as she headed to her apartment. Scott and Hyena would probably ramp up the screwing tonight just to prove a point. Hazel slammed the door and locked it behind her while texting Claire with the details of her elevator ride right away.

It had been a frustrating night—from top to bottom. But thinking about Wolf's bottom was at the top of her frustration list right now. She wanted to take out her loneliness on him. Between her legs. Even if she was pissed at him for stealing her money.

The physical contact she'd had with Wolf tonight had her all fired up, clearly burning through her common sense in a hot minute. Maybe she even wanted to have him not stop at the kissing. It was a blow, actually, that she hadn't been the one to send him away.

It was a weird night that she decided to put to bed after she had a nice hot shower.

XOXOXOXO

In the morning, well the late morning, she got a text message from Claire.

I'm here. I'm coming up.

Claire had a key and all her codes because she was Hazel's person. So Claire was sitting on the end of her bed, offering a cup of coffee from their favorite shop, before Hazel even got to have her morning pee.

Hazel fluffed the pillows and sat up in bed, taking the cup from her friend. Then Claire sat next to her.

"So what color do you want to wear?"

They both took sips of their coffee.

"To what?" Hazel was confused and looked at Claire's face. Her eyes were shining with excitement.

"My wedding. You're the maid of honor, of course."

"What the hell happened last night?" Hazel touched the back of her head, which actually hurt a little. Whether it was from the hangover or the blow she took to it, she wasn't sure.

"Him. He happened. We're getting married as soon as humanly possible. Well, as soon as possible while looking fabulous in a splendid venue. He proposed. I said yes." Claire held out her left hand, which appeared to have a paperclip wrapped around it.

"You haven't even known him a full day." Hazel set her coffee on her nightstand and turned to face Claire, grabbing her by the shoulders.

"It doesn't matter. He's the one. I know it better than I know my name. You know how it is with me and you? How we just get each other? He's like that, but with a beautiful penis, and I love him so much." Claire pulled her phone out of her pocket and squealed. "He'll be here in a minute."

"You've lost your mind." Hazel watched as her friend bounded to the intercom and buzzed up someone.

"Please." Claire went from excited to serious. "Be supportive. You know my family will be against this."

"Yes. Because they are sane." Hazel pulled the covers up over her sleep tank just as a knock on the door made her long for more clothes.

"You know, if you could just be the person who understands this, that's what I need right now." Claire left her to answer the door.

Hazel leaned over the bed, grabbed the robe she had tossed on the floor after her shower last night, and was able to get her arms in it and put her nipples away before Chance and Claire came into her bedroom, canoodling again.

"Hazel?" Chance addressed her.

Hazel covered her mouth, grateful that the coffee probably masked her morning hangover breath but still self-conscious.

"I wanted someone to witness this." The huge man dropped to his knee and grabbed Claire's hand. He wiggled the paperclip off and pulled a blue box from his pocket. "I know we covered this last night, but I wanted to make it very official. Claire, I've been waiting for you. My whole life. You make everything clear. Be my wife."

Claire teared up and nodded furiously as Chance slipped a sparkling ring on her finger. Hazel felt her own eyes moisten.

It was not normal to fall in love in less than twelve hours, but the way Chance looked at Claire was something to see.

Hazel belted her robe and crawled out of bed. After Chance stood to kiss and hug Claire, Hazel stepped into their embrace.

"You crazy kids. I'm so happy for you."

Chance picked them both up in his excitement, and Claire and Hazel screamed and laughed.

Claire was getting married. *Damn.*

Yeah, You Can't Just Marry People Like That

Wolf got into work on time, and as soon as he noticed Chance was missing, he checked his phone. As if his best friend heard the question on the waves of telepathic bromance, a text popped up with a picture.

It was a picture of an engagement ring.

Oh shit.

Wolf texted back:

Yeah, you can't just marry people like that.

Chance got him back immediately.

Like hell I can't. She's perfection. PS, I'm going to be late, brother.

This was bad. Chance was losing his mind. Granted, Claire was gorgeous and their energies were synched up, but to be cautious, they should really make sure their energies didn't change over a period of time.

He pushed his phone into his pocket. He would have to

worry about that later. Right now he was taking updates on the second string of singles coming in tonight. His first priority was matching anyone from last night. String A had to be sorted and satisfied, and then he worked on the next list. They usually got through three whole groups before moving to the next city.

His staff was issuing the invites for a mixer very similar to the one they held last night. He had six snapshots of leftover singles who just didn't work with anyone else.

He shuffled until he got to her, though he told himself it was just paperwork. She was the most dissatisfied client last night, so they would work hard tonight to get her matched up. None of the leftover men from last night were a match, so she would be the first up to bat when he was matching tonight.

He would find a great match, and she would be done complaining and fighting with him. He put her picture in the top drawer of his desk.

Chance walked in three hours late with a big, dumb grin on his face. He picked up Wolf when he saw him. "She said yes! Holy shit!"

"You asked her already? Put me down, you goddamned monster." Wolf pushed free.

"I did. She was into it. You're my best man. We're getting married as soon as possible. You know what? This place is gorgeous! We have it for what? Eight weeks? Maybe we can do the ceremony here."

Chance gestured around the room like he was seeing it for the first time.

"It's great. And this is where we met. How romantic. Can

you believe it, brother? I'm doing it. It's happening."

"You met her yesterday."

"That was a great damn day." Chance touched the painting Hazel had stolen for a little while the night before. "This stuff is gorgeous. It would make a great wedding venue, right? She said yes. I can't believe it. We've done this for over two years, and I believed in it for everyone else, but I never thought of it for me. You know? But now that it's happened, I want to dip your whole body in solid gold; because of you, there is her. You are epic. Damn it, I love you." Chance slapped Wolf into a hug again.

His friend's exuberance was contagious, and Wolf could feel a smirk working on his lips. "I love you, too, you impulsive girl."

Chance picked Wolf up the way Wolf had carried Hazel yesterday and started singing, "I feel pretty! Oh so pretty!"

The staff had gathered around the spectacle his friend was putting on and including him in.

"We have work to do, dickhead. Let's go."

Chance was a happy idiot, but he normally had a pretty impressive work ethic. Luckily, the mention of the job seemed to snap Chance out of his delirium. After he set Wolf down for the second time, Chance had to clear up one thing.

"You'll do it, right? You'll be my best man?"

Wolf rolled his eyes before slapping Chance's huge back. "Of course. You know I'll do it."

The staff started clapping until Wolf shooed them back to their posts.

Wolf didn't show it, but he was worried about this sudden relationship, which was ironic considering his line of work.

Chance didn't give his heart freely. He was always aloof with the ladies. But he was so head over heels, Wolf was afraid if it didn't work out, if the energy—soured, Chance would blame him.

Back At It Again

Luna, the Booty Camp staff who called Hazel to tell her about the second night of meetings at the theater, was in the right line of work. She was very convincing. Claire was with Hazel and helped push her over the edge, telling her that she was going to spend time with Chance—who had been texting her all day—and they would go together.

Luna said that Wolf had a few dates in mind for her—which hurt Hazel's feelings a lot after the kiss they'd shared—and he would be open to discussing the refund she wanted.

Claire was convinced Wolf was a decent guy because Chance spoke fondly of the man in the hours they were together. And she thought maybe the call was bait to bring Hazel back so he could kiss her again.

Hazel's body wanted another kiss, but her brain was highly opposed to the idea. After going through her closet with Claire, Hazel picked a soft, black sheath dress and boots. Her warm jacket would be an improvement on last night's getup. She pulled her hair into a tight bun, and Claire made fun of her for looking like a librarian.

They stopped at Claire's apartment on the way back to the theater, and she spent a very long time getting dressed for her new fiancé. Hazel took two Advil and lay on the couch to catch a nap while she waited.

Eventually Claire shook her awake, all hyped up on her excitement, and Hazel felt a knot in her stomach. She tried to tell herself it was because she would be in the meat market environment again. But she knew the real deal was her anticipation at seeing Wolf. Would he act differently after the kiss? He'd done it because he felt bad for her. But he sure as hell had committed to the playacting. Maybe he looked down on the Booty Camp clients? Did he think they were desperate and beneath him?

As she worked her way up the tiny steps of the theater, she wet her lips. And checked her hair in the reflection in the glass door. No stray pieces seemed to be escaping. Then his face was on the other side as he opened the door for her.

His forearms were particularly distracting, as was his cologne, as she scooted through the door and pushed through the second set of doors.

He didn't greet them, but Chance made them feel welcome with his huge smile. Obviously, the few hours apart had made Claire and Chance even fonder for each other, and he pulled her in for an exuberant kiss. "It's been forever since I did that last."

Claire sighed happily and agreed.

Wolf had on an exact replica of the Booty Camp staff T-shirt that Hazel had folded and placed at the end of her bed this morning. She handed him the jacket she had borrowed.

He was standing next to her and seemed to find a set of

manners in his body somewhere because he asked, "How you feeling today?"

"A little used, honestly. You took my money, and you're holding it hostage. And then the elevator last night..." she trailed off, not wanting to admit to what they had done with the other staff lingering around.

"You know the deal with the money. It's the weekend, so the banks aren't going to even be working toward clearing your grandma-style check." He gestured to a staff member across the lobby. "Okay. Off to find the poor bastard who winds up with you."

She gave his retreating back the finger again. This fucking guy. His pity kisses and bad attitude were grinding on her last nerve.

The scene at Booty Camp was a repeat of the one from the previous night. Claire had to part from her new man when he started his spiel from the evening before with his characteristic gusto. It was altered a bit to acknowledge the clients that had been present last night, too.

"Do we have to sit through the whole speech inside again?" Hazel asked.

"I don't want to miss a word of it. Chance has so much passion." Claire hooked her arm in Hazel's and they brought up the rear as the crowd filed into the seats.

While they waited for everyone to settle, Claire leaned over and whispered, "Wolf can't take his eyes off you." She discreetly pointed to the seat where Wolf had sat last night. He had a folder with him this time, and sure enough, when they made eye contact, he narrowed his eyes at her.

"That's because he hates me." Hazel gave him a matching

glower.

"I think if you two recorded yourselves hate fucking, you could make about four million dollars. The chemistry popping off you guys is bonkers." Claire made a rude gesture with her hands.

Hazel covered Claire's naughty hands with one of her own. "Stop. We have no chemistry. He's evil."

"What about the kiss last night? How was it?" Claire pouted and made kissy noises.

"I already told you." Hazel used her other hand to cover Claire's mouth.

Claire started wiggling her eyebrows.

"It was hot, but it was a charity kiss."

Claire freed her hands and uncovered her mouth. "Did Scott and Hyena see it, though?"

"Oh yeah. That part was badass." Hazel bit her lip and turned toward the stage now that Chance was finally looking serious about speaking.

"Wolf did a nice thing, though. Right?" Claire seemed intent on improving Hazel's impression of Chance's best friend.

"He's setting me up on dates tonight, so I don't think I rocked his world. He's mean, anyway." Hazel pretended to dust off her shoulder to show Claire how little she cared.

"Oh. I didn't know that. I'm sorry, honey." Claire patted Hazel's leg.

Chance started in on how his name should be everyone's mantra for the evening—take a chance.

Claire whispered in Hazel's ear, "I'm going to take so much of Chance in my throat tonight I'll gag on it."

Hazel could feel a smile start despite her fairly shitty mood. "You're a filthy animal, Claire."

"If I get enough wine in me, I'll be the filthiest animal that has ever been in that man's bed." Claire made her hands into claws and growled.

Wolf tapped them both on the shoulder as Chance dismissed the crowd. It was matchmaking time.

"You're my priority tonight, Hazel. You get matched up first." She could see the tattoo on his forearm in her peripheral vision. It made her heart race.

She wanted him to say he was her match. Where that thought came from, she wasn't sure, but her heart was hoping he wanted to kiss her again. That the kiss in the elevator had been as good for him as it'd been for her.

"I have a guy who might work out for you. Which is a goddamned miracle, considering your felonious tendencies." Wolf took his hand away, and she and Claire stood.

"You into role play, Wolfie? She's the prisoner and you're the warden?" Claire fake-boxed him as Chance came up behind her. He put his hands on his new fiancée's hips.

Hazel felt her own blush and spied a faint one on Wolf's cheeks, as well.

"Hazel's match is right over there. Tonight can count as the first date in the contract's fine print contract. You might as well get a head start. If you knock out those five dates and manage to not find your soul mate, then you can get your money back."

Hazel wasn't sure if she was more angry that he was pointing her toward another man or insinuating that getting her a refund without her having to pimp herself out would take so long.

"It takes ten days for your bank to clear the check, right? I think I'd rather wait." Hazel refused to look in the direction of the man she was due to be set up with.

"Well, it takes ten business days, and you know next week is a bank holiday on Monday. After your check clears, I'll write you a refund check. Does your bank have a hold period for large funds, too?" Wolf looked down at his clipboard while she realized if he refunded her money with a check, her bank would also hold it for ten days.

"You devious bastard. Just refund it in cash." Hazel was feeling her anger rise.

Wolf looked up and seemed to take a second to stare at her before responding. "You complete five dates that I match? And they *all* fail? *And* you report directly to me why they fail? I'll take a chance on your check actually not bouncing and refund you cash." He stepped closer. "And you have to give them a real shot. I have to agree that the reason not to date the guy is valid."

Hazel stepped into his personal space and poked him in the chest. "Fine. Do your best, Booty Camp Overlord. And if you set me up with a serial killer..."

Claire filled in the usual threat that Hazel had used on her in the past. "She'll haunt you and all of your descendants forever after she's dead."

"Fair enough. Go meet Brent. He's a contractor. Self-made man. Great match. Don't be a bitch." Wolf pointed to a guy in a nice suit holding a drink.

Chance kissed Claire's cheek and held out an elbow to

Hazel. She growled at Wolf as she passed and let Chance take her to the new guy. As they got closer she realized Brent's hair had frosted blond tips.

Chance made the introductions, and Brent had a nice smile that didn't quite reach his eyes as he held out his hand to Hazel.

"Feel free to kiss the ring."

Hazel noticed Brent had a large gold pinkie ring on the hand he was offering her to shake.

"I'm good. Thanks."

Chance left them to have their "date."

Hazel could almost feel Wolf staring at the back of her head.

It's Fine

Wolf watched Hazel's stiff body language with Brent and smiled internally. Brent wasn't making a good impression. After finding three guys in the room who had great energies for Hazel, Wolf picked a guy who couldn't be worse for her. He had no rational explanation for it.

It wasn't like his palms itched to touch her the second Hazel had shimmied past him coming in the theater door. It wasn't like her gorgeous face was highlighted by the severe bun she wore. Or the fact that he spent a good ten minutes trying to decide which way he liked her hair better—soft and loose or high on her head.

Okay, he maybe had a huge crush on her, but she was a client and seemed like a bitch. He'd deal with the attraction with some vigorous self-love for the next seven or so weeks or find a nice girl who wasn't involved with Booty Camp at all. No dating clients was his rule. Strictly enforced. The customers had to feel safe and trust them, and if the staff was hitting on all the singles who walked in the door, his whole business would become a joke.

At least no one was on to him.

Wolf excused himself from Claire and went back to his office to avoid seeing Hazel with Brent.

He hadn't even sat down for a moment when Chance walked in and closed the door behind him. "Well, you have a huge boner for Hazel. What the hell is up?"

Wolf tossed up his hands and leaned back in his chair. "Oh, fuck you."

"Okay, I'm no professional matchmaker, but I've learned some shit here with you. Chemistry between you and Hazel? Off the charts. Chemistry between her and that doorknob out there? Not even there. I think she may even punch him before the night is over. You always pair douchebags with hollow sluts. And they work out great." Chance sat on top of the old desk, and it groaned from his huge weight.

"Don't break the desk, Hulk." Wolf swatted at Chance with the folder on his desk.

Chance didn't move. "Explain yourself."

"Go outside and mack on your new woman and leave me be. I know what I'm doing. Hazel is a pain in the ass and will be a tough person to match. She needs to learn what she hates first. You know I do that sometimes." Wolf opened up his folder next to Chance's giant thigh and tried to focus on who his B matches would be tonight.

"Do you know what she does for a living?" Chance wasn't leaving just yet.

"Yeah. She's a teacher. She likes bossing people around. Probably has control issues." He pulled out the picture of Brent. This one *would* actually be the tough match. Wolf didn't like his energy at all. But he took money from everyone. Even assholes.

75

"She's a special education teacher." Chance stood then.

Wolf looked at his lap. *Shit.* His sister, Faith, had had special needs, and she'd passed away at eighteen. He loved her so much with all of his heart. The tattoo that wrapped around his forearm was a stylized version of his sister's favorite cartoon dragon. He missed Faith every day. Chance knew this.

"Low blow," was all he had to say.

Chance put a huge hand on Wolf's shoulder. "You seem to have a preconceived notion about her, and you're normally always right about people. But as far as I'm concerned, anyone who does that job every day can't be written off."

With that, his best friend left.

Wolf touched his tattoo. He wanted to go out and kiss Hazel again right now. Pull her away from Brent and into his arms. In front of everyone. Which was, of course, the last thing he could allow himself to do.

It was like wishing for her made her appear. She was angry, and she didn't bother to knock before she flung open his door. "You ass clown."

Set Up By A Maniac With A Maniac

Hazel caught the office door before it bounced back and hit her, and then she slammed it shut. "You think you're some sort of matchmaker? What the living hell is going on in your brain? You're a maniac and you set me up with a maniac."

Wolf shook his head. "You burned through that one quick. Tell me why he didn't work for you?"

"Oh, is this part of the contractually obligated after-date rundown? Because you have to decide if I can make up my own mind, you sexist pig?" She curled her hands into fists.

"What does that even mean?" He gestured to the chair across from him.

"You're a professional matchmaker, correct?" She took the seat and glowered at him and his long lashes and stupid high cheekbones.

"I run this business, if that's what you're asking." Wolf twirled a pen between his fingers.

"Okay, in what world does a guy start a conversation by asking me to kiss his ring? And then proceed to tell me how he got a blow job at a gas station last week and almost got arrested for it, which would have been bad because the girl doing the sucking was married. How do you think that would go down with my dad? When I introduced them?"

Wolf put down the pen and drummed his fingers. "Okay, that's a fair point. I wouldn't recommend any guy saying that to a woman on a first date."

"Date? That wasn't a date. That was eight minutes of my life I'll never get back. It did, ironically make me eight hundred percent madder at you. So there's that." She leaned forward, ready to pounce on Wolf.

"So you don't consider that a date? Then you still have five left. Fine by me." Wolf gave her a slow smile.

"Oh, that counts as two. Because I want to go home and take a long hot shower to get the way he looked at me out of my mind." She shivered.

Wolf seemed angry for a second but then acquiesced. "Fine. That one counts for two."

"Finally, you agree to something."

Hazel's cell phone vibrated in her pocket. She pulled it out and was completely puzzled because she was getting a call from Scott. "What the hell? Why is my dickbag ex calling me?" She said it to herself, yet out loud, and answered with a tentative, "Hello?"

"Hey. What are you up to?" Scott sounded chill. Well, maybe a little nervous, she switched him to speakerphone by accident. Her phone locked her out, but the call continued.

"Why are you calling me, Scott?" Hazel stood and turned away from Wolf to try and get some privacy.

"I just wanted to know what you were up to."

"My life. I'm up to living my life. Which doesn't include you unless I have to cover my ears while you bang the laughing hyena on my ceiling."

Hazel heard Wolf's chair scrape on the floor and his footfalls come up behind her.

"I miss you. Seeing you last night with that dirtbag made me miss you." Scott cleared his throat.

Wolf was behind her and made a disgusted noise. Hazel turned, and if she'd liked Wolf, she could have easily hugged him—he was that close. He offered his opinion on Scott.

"That guy just wants what he can't have." Wolf looked angry.

And that made Hazel want to drop the phone and Wolf's pants at the same time. What the hell was it about this guy that got her so fired up?

"Is he with you right now? You know he's just after a little local tail. I saw him on TV earlier today. He works at the Booty Camp. I mean, talk about being a desperate loser. He's setting people up at a dating factory? Anyway, I wanted to warn you and see what you're doing later." Scott cleared his throat again.

"I'm seriously confused right now. You have a girlfriend." Hazel made eye contact with Wolf.

"That doesn't mean you and I can't be friends with benefits. I know how to make things work for you, if you know what I mean." Scott dropped his voice an octave. His sex voice.

Wolf snatched the phone out of her hand.

"Scott? Your name is Scott? Why am I not surprised? Every Scott I've ever met was a self-absorbed mama's boy. Yes, I'm with her. No, she won't be around later, so stick your dick in a garbage disposal and turn it the fuck on, how about that?" Wolf ended the call and held out her phone to her.

"Why'd you do that?" She accepted it back and tucked it in her folded arms.

He ran his hand through his hair and then scratched his chin. "Um. You needed help. It's just a Booty Camp service. Ridding clients of unhealthy exes."

"So is that why you kissed me like I was the last woman on the planet last night? A service?" She lifted her eyebrows and waited for his response.

"I told you. I didn't want him being a jerk to you. Until you're not our client anymore, your love life is my concern. And I don't want your match screwed up by blasts from the past." Wolf went back behind his desk.

Hazel went over to it and put her hands on top of the papers he was pretending to read. "But it's okay to make me talk to that guy out there who saw fit to put his penis into our very first conversation? That's okay?"

Wolf thought for a second and then shook his head once.

"Well, he's out there with the next match making her life miserable, I'm sure. So you better step up to the plate and go out there and kiss her for her own good. Just like you did to me last night." Hazel walked over to the door and pulled it open. "Go on now."

She waited, knowing she'd caught him. He'd kissed her last night out of some odd sense of pity, but he'd made her date someone else not fifteen minutes ago. It wasn't fair.

Wolf stood up and walked past her, eyeing her like she might explode, and then went to find Brent, the blond-tipped penis talker.

He must have mentioned something to Chance on the way over because they were a pair by the time they were escorting Brent out the front door. Brent started cursing and fighting while Chance promised they would refund the man's money.

After the man had been set outside the theater, Wolf walked back to his office and bowed to her. She was leaning against the doorjamb.

"Happy now?"

"No. For Pete's sake, that guy harasses me and gets his money back! You're incredible." She gave him double middle fingers and pushed past him. She wasn't waiting for him to escort her home—or anyone else, for that matter.

Well, There She Goes

He watched her leave and felt the regret of seeing her go. He wasn't allowed to harbor that feeling for her at all. She was a client. And he could hear his mother and grandmother's warnings about the state of his karma because he was monetizing the family "gift."

They'd warned him about his marriage. That he was forcing it to prove them wrong. And after his wife left, he'd spent an entire month drunk. They'd been right.

Chance had pulled Wolf out of his house and forced him to go back to work. There were too many people waiting for their happy endings for him to give up. The irony was vivid.

He pulled Hazel's picture out of the desk. He'd set her up with a man he knew wouldn't work out. Instead of the clearly nice guys who had very complementary resumes and energies.

Wolf wouldn't think about why he was sabotaging her. Or refusing to refund her money when he could clearly cover the cost. Booty Camp was a national sensation. He even had to hire someone to watch his money and manage his investments. He simply didn't have the time that kind of money required.

Chance knocked on the open door, his new fiancée trailing behind and then breaking the silence.

"Where's Hazel?"

"She left. She's going to have to go on a weekday date now to meet the terms of her fine print." Wolf tucked her picture back in the desk without either of them noticing what he was looking at.

Claire pulled her phone out of her purse. "She texted me."

She left the office after giving Wolf a dirty look, obviously trying to make a phone call.

Chance took the seat Hazel had vacated just minutes before. "Okay. Let's talk about the Wednesday night dates. I think we're going to have a hell of a crowd out there tonight. Lots of B matches. Almost like your head wasn't in the game—if I was going to hazard a guess."

His huge friend cracked his knuckles.

"My head is fine. Some cases are harder than others. We'll do a B match night on Tuesday. I'll spend time with the pictures between now and then. It'll be fine." Wolf took the list Chance pulled out of his pocket.

"All of these were unsatisfactory?" Wolf was surprised. There was easily double the amount of people who normally had to go on another date. It was troubling.

"Yeah. Maybe you should go on a date before you do your next session. Get rid of some of this block you have all of a sudden." Chance stood as Claire entered the room and ended her call.

"Well, she's almost home. She's not a huge fan of yours, I gotta say." She slid next to Chance and wrapped her arm around his waist.

When they were together, the energy between them almost glittered. They would work out. And then Wolf came to the crushing realization that he would most likely be leaving his best friend in Garville when Booty Camp ambled on to the next tour date.

"Yeah. Okay. Give out the information we need the clients to have. Then you crazy kids can get the hell out of here and spend some time together." Wolf waved them out the door.

Chance being in mad, crazy love for the first time in his life would most likely free up Wolf to wallow in his own head drama without interference.

He shuffled the pictures in front of him and tried to make some new matches. He forced himself to pull out her picture from last night. The too-tight top and the wild hair were amazing, but tonight's version of Hazel seemed much closer to her personality. And he spent way too much time imagining unwinding her long hair from the tight bun she wore than was good for him.

And There's Scott

Hazel got out of the cab she'd managed to snag when she stormed out of Booty Camp. She was so done with hanging out and waiting to find out that everyone had a perfect match besides her. Honestly, she couldn't get her money back, but when she looked at the reviews for the business online, they were all aces. Love-struck fools would not stop going on about how successful the camp was.

So her heart had started some stupid hoping. Wishing, even. That maybe instead of getting her money back in a timely fashion, she might even get the man of her dreams. She pictured telling her grandchildren that she'd found their thousand-dollar grandpa. Or that he still owed her a thousand dollars. Whatever. Something cute.

As she jabbed the button to call the elevator, she thought about the kiss Wolf had laid on her the night before. And his protective response to Scott on the phone.

She sighed. She could even make the literally foolproof Booty Camp equation crap its pants.

The doors slid open to reveal Scott in jeans and a tank. With his guns out. Damn it. She had a weakness for arms and armpit hair. It was all very sexual. And he knew it. In their five-month relationship, she'd often told him how much she liked the look on him.

He hit her with his best smolder. "Hey, baby."

She stepped to the side so he could get out and gestured with her hand for him to vacate.

"Nope. I'm going up. Just had to switch my laundry from the washer to the dryer."

He caught the door and held it open for her.

She had no other choice but to get on the elevator with him.

"So, your new boyfriend is possessive as shit, huh?" Scott was standing too close.

"He's not my boyfriend." She looked at the elevator buttons and wondered if she pressed the button again and again, would the elevator go faster.

"Is that so? Tara's not here tonight. If you know what I mean." Scott bumped her shoulder with his.

She'd told this man she loved him less than three months ago. Her body still remembered what he could do to it. But her brain remembered that he was doing those same things to another body, too.

Hazel stepped out on her floor, and he followed her. "You live upstairs."

Scott followed her all the way to her door. "I know. I just wanted to make sure that you know."

Hazel was more than confused by this sudden swing in Scott's attitude. Maybe he always needed a piece on the side? She unlocked her door, stepped into her apartment, and closed the door in his face.

She ignored his knock and texted Claire that Scott had followed her. It was insane.

Claire made sure to remind her what a douchebag Scott was. And that a quickie to relieve stress wasn't worth the emotional attachment. And she was right. Hazel knew she was worth more than that. Even if she was such a problem that she'd burned through her first date at Booty Camp in less than two minutes. In a place where people were guaranteed to find a match. Claire went to her closet and changed into short shorts and a sleep tank. Saturday was a dead deal.

In the mirror, she unraveled her hair from the bun she had it in. It had great volume. She shook it out, grimacing at the weird hair pain that followed that type of style.

Her cell phone rang. It was a number she didn't recognize. Maybe Hyena had a landline and Scott was calling her from that.

She let it roll to voice mail as she got under her fluffy white comforter. Then Hazel hit the button to listen to the message on speakerphone. It was Wolf.

"Listen, Hazel. Claire just told me that your ex-boyfriend was sniffing around. I just wanted to make sure you were still single. You can't get your money back if you're dating or involved with someone. It's not fair to the other clients. Okay. Just so we're clear."

That call ended, and her voice mail started auto playing unintentionally saved messages. Ironically, the next one was an old one from Scott.

"Hey, baby. Just wanted to let you know I need to see you tonight. Wear the good sex clothes."

The date stamp on this one was from the night they broke up. He'd known he was going to break her heart. Scott heard her say that she was in love with him, and still made sure he finished.

Men sucked. In her messages, she had one telling her not to be a disappointment, and another getting ready for his big date to disappoint her. Because she wasn't enough.

It was not a great night as she curled around her phone and tried her best to go to sleep.

And W♡rk ♡n M♡nday

Working as an elementary special education teacher was a saving grace. After spending Sunday in her pajamas, Hazel was ready for work on Monday.

The needs in front of her were so immediate and varied she couldn't wallow in her own pity party.

She had six students, and each needed something different. Mackenzie had autism and was working hard with her task board. She loved to spend time on the classroom's computer as a reward. Jonah was in a wheelchair and had limited mobility. Hazel was perfecting a program that would work with the tray on his wheelchair and his right hand to help him communicate. Teaching Mackenzie, Jonah, and their other classmates life skills along with their modified curriculum was a filling day. An exhausting one that was challenging and rewarding. It took limitless patience, which Hazel surely didn't have in all aspects of her life, but in this classroom, she could always tap into her inner calm to be what the kids needed.

Unlike the other teachers who got a planning period every day, her students needed her all day save for her thirty-minute lunch break when the school nurse and a paraeducator would step in and help the kids eat their meals.

And that's when Claire snagged her on Monday. On her way to the teachers' lounge for some food and a quick bathroom break. "Come eat your boring salad in my office. We have to talk wedding plans."

Hazel used the office bathroom before sitting down in the comfy chair in Claire's corner setup where parents often sat. The wall was papered with drawings of Claire and for Claire from the students. She recognized a new one that looked like it was Mackenzie's favorite style. "That from my girl?" Hazel pointed with her fork.

"Yes. I was going to tell you about it. A bird."

Hazel had figured that out. "Of course." Mackenzie's favorite thing in life was birds. So it was a huge compliment to Claire that Kenzie had gifted her with one, even if it was made out of wax and paper.

"And before you ask—yes, I had her make eye contact when she was speaking. So formal. But she went out of her normal routine to give it to me in the lobby this morning." Claire smiled.

Success. Working in a school where almost all the staff was on board with helping the kids reach their personal goals was really helpful in her kids' development.

"Thank you." Hazel smiled back.

"You don't have to thank me. I should be thanking you. I love to see the progress your kids make, nice and steady. You've got a talent, lady." Claire started looking at her engagement ring again.

Hazel slipped right into the next conversation. "You still excited?"

It seemed like the right question to ask; she didn't want Claire to think she was anything but supportive. Especially after the beautiful pep talk Claire had just lathered all over her.

"It's been the best weekend of my life. He's so much more than just the talking head at Booty Camp. He has dreams, and he's the first man I've ever dated who wasn't threatened by how focused I am with my career. I mean, usually they either think I finger-paint all day or I'll make the best wife ever because the kids they want me to crank out will listen to me." Claire shook her head and touched her ring once more.

"Aren't you going to eat?" Hazel took another bite of her Cobb salad.

"Already did. Couldn't take it anymore. I had so much sex this weekend I was starving."

"Good for you." Hazel tried not to be bitter about all the sex she wasn't getting.

"Listen, Wolf was super upset that Scott was hitting on you." Claire took her ring off and put it back on and pulled it off again.

"I know. He left a message. Told me if I damaged the goods with a non-Booty Camp approved date, I wouldn't get my money back. This whole scene is a little too eighteenth century for me." Hazel tossed her salad with her fork.

"That's crazy. He was pissed because he was jealous. I could tell." Claire put her ring on and left it while she tapped her fingernails on her desk blotter. "I swore he was going to call you for a date."

"Hardly. He gave me one pity kiss. And now he's just a nitwit. That guy he set me up with got *his* money back! Because he was being creepy. Maybe I need to talk about my penis more to people." Hazel paused in her tirade to take a drink from her water bottle.

"Well, Chance thinks you and Wolf are a good match. He said Wolf is a really great friend, and he has issues beyond his control. Basically, he said he sets up a ton of happy endings but thinks he'll never get one himself." Claire pulled her lips to one side in a grimace.

"I will say he knows how to kiss, but Chance is projecting this stuff on Wolf and me. The man hates me." Hazel looked at Kenzie's picture again. The girl was working hard on the feathers on her birds, which was great for her fine motor skills.

"Speaking of hate, Tuesday is the next Booty Camp session. It's a more staff-involved date situation where you and your match get assistance from a professional to explore your similar interests." Claire shook her mouse and the screen came to life with a picture of her and Chance outside of the theater.

"You move fast." Hazel nodded to the screen.

"You have no idea. I'm like a puma in the bedroom." Claire pretended to twerk in her chair.

Hazel replied, "I was eating."

"Okay, so Tuesday night, wear your favorite perfume. I'll be coming with you because I'll get to hang out with Chance during any off time he gets. He said this usually seals the deal for the first round, and then they'll start the process again until it's time for the Booty Camp tour to move on." Claire pulled up an email that had almost those exact words on it. As if she'd memorized the thing.

"What will you and Chance do? Where does he go next?" Hazel closed up her Tupperware with her fork inside and worked on the rest of her water.

Claire sighed. "He goes to Townola next. And that's over two hours away. We're not sure how we're going to manage. I know we have to get married in the next month, so tomorrow we'll start the process in order to get the paperwork filed in time."

Hazel wasn't sure how Claire could commit to a relationship without having a clear plan to see one another on a regular basis. It all seemed rushed. They'd known each other for one weekend.

"He's the one for me. When you know, you just know." Claire spoke with the dreamy afterglow of a teenager in love.

Hazel looked at the clock. She had to meet her kiddos in the cafeteria so she could go outside with them for recess. Kenzie needed to be coached on making friends, and Jonah loved to be put in the swing designed specifically for kids in wheelchairs.

"I've got to run."

"Can I tell Chance you'll be there Tuesday? He wants to make sure your match is perfect." Claire stood as well, clearly headed to another part of her busy day.

Hazel thought of how she went to bed curled around her phone on Saturday. She hated that she was being forced into these dates, but she really didn't have a choice. She wanted her money back. "Yeah, give him the okay."

Claire looked a little too pleased with herself, which gave

Hazel the impression that her friend was up to something.

ShE May HavE T♡ld HiM

Wolf had Googled Scott to no avail. He needed the asshat's last name to make any headway on his stalking. He'd figured out what had bothered him so much about the guy. It was his energy. It was off. He certainly wasn't a match to Hazel—that was the truth.

And Claire had told him way too much about the details of the ending of their relationship.

That the Ken doll had left her after screwing her—*and* made sure to keep his beer cold while he literally fucked her over for the last time—made Wolf want to punch pretty much everything and everyone.

Hazel was a fucking gorgeous girl. Just stunning. Her lips were made for kissing, nice and slow and then desperate and quick. When he'd taken her in the elevator and held her body against his, he'd known she would not be a disappointment naked. Her breasts were the perfect size. And her ass had just enough give that he could get two handfuls of it.

Jesus he was getting hard just thinking about her. Her energy when she was at the peak of her pleasure would be a thing to behold. Wasted on a guy who took the time to trim his armpit hair or whatever that dude did to jingle his bells.

He was getting so fired up he was starting to picture stuff with her. Holding her. Brushing her hair away from her face. And these were dangerous thoughts. Because as difficult as it was to have his wife leave him, he'd always known they didn't work. His grandmother and mother were right. He'd tried to force it, force fate to give him what he wanted.

But with Hazel? She was like a magnet. He felt drawn to her, watching her face get angry with him. Seeing her eyes flash and her cheeks blush.

He was absolutely positive that the hurt he would feel if he fell for Hazel would slay him. Of course, he could be wrong. But too many people relied on him to grant their deepest wishes for him to start worrying about himself. And then there were all the people he employed. They needed these jobs.

He looked down at the pictures again, holding Hazel above the eligible bachelors. Wolf closed his eyes for a second to clear them of his own prejudices. There was a guy in the pile who would do great. Hazel and Greg would make a great couple. If they decided to have kids, they would be gorgeous.

He touched his tattoo again, thinking of his sister. Being eight years older made him part sibling, part parent. He'd met many teachers over the years, going to the open houses and looking at her desk or her art with her.

His eyes welled up when he thought of her trusting hand in his as she took him down the hallways.

"It's a good desk, Wolfie. Wanna sit in it?"

He'd helped her with her favorite doll's hair more times than he could count. She would wait for him and critique his technique to tease him. But her happiness when all the knots were out was worth sitting for hours.

At fourteen, she was held back a year, so she was in middle school but she was still a young girl in her mind, he'd had to intervene on her behalf. A group of boys had taken a liking to gather in the parking lot of the school for recess, and they had a knack for getting Faith alone to tease her.

At twenty-two, he had been far too old to fight middle school battles, but he tracked his sister to the pavement where the kids spent their free time to watch it go down after she had mentioned it to him the night before. There was a little patch of wildflowers next to the overgrown tennis courts where Faith went to sit. She would pick a few and pretend they were acting out scenes in her head. She did it at home all the time when he was working outside at his mother's house.

The boys came at her in a clump of eight, looking like they might be friendly, but Wolf caught their energies. Malice. He wondered if Faith had even been able to understand what they said to her.

He exited his vehicle and trotted over to his sister. The boys didn't even see him coming. Faith lit up when she saw him, getting to her feet and offering him the flowers she'd been playing with as a gift. She was so generous.

Her holding two crumpled wildflowers broke him. Her innocence and tender soul were too raw in this setting where she was obviously being preyed on.

He hugged his sister and took the flowers before he kissed the top of her head and sent her back to school. After he tucked the flowers in the pocket of his jeans, he faced her tormentors.

As it became obvious to the boys that this was going to end badly for them, he smiled.

When his sister was out of sight, he chuckled. "Hey, guys. Just want to make this clear."

And he knew he was out of bounds right then. A twenty-two-year-old man threatening thirteen-year-old kids wasn't cool at all. Not even a little bit. But it didn't stop him.

"Faith is not your friend. And she's not a toy for you assholes to use."

The boys were caught. Instinct made them want to listen to an elder, but they knew they should probably run.

"I'm going to remember each one of you. From this moment and for the rest of your goddamned lives. If I even see you near my sister again, I will beat the living shit out of you. I promise. Do you understand?"

Wolf stepped closer to the group of them.

Some apologized while some laughed nervously.

"I'm crazy. So you know. And I love her more than anything. I'll go to jail in a hot minute just to teach any of you little bitches a lesson."

There was no more nervous giggling as he looked from one to the next.

After that scene, he fully expected to get arrested. But Wolf never had to pay for defending his sister that day. Nor did those kids go near her again.

Of course, he made sure to drive by at recess time until she was promoted to high school.

But for Faith, he couldn't be rational. Losing her four years later was more than he could take. He missed her every day.

He even still had the flowers from that day long ago. They were saved in a Ziploc bag where they were dry. He kept them by his favorite picture of Faith with her friend. The earth wasn't good enough for his sister. But he would have fought to make it what she needed if he were still lucky enough to have her.

He wiped a tear off of his cheek. This happened when he missed her. It probably always would.

Chance knocked on the office door, and Wolf focused on the pictures. He handed the Polaroid to his manager.

"All matched up?" Chance shuffled through the pictures until he got to Hazel and flipped it towards him. "Even this one?"

"It's sorted. Run with it." Wolf looked back down to his desk.

"Okay, brother," Chance replied with a hint of disapproval.

ThEy Will WɵRK This TimE

Hazel picked out a less formal outfit tonight. Jeans, a white blouse, and boots with her hair down. Claire was on her way over for some pre-drinking drinks, so Hazel got out two wine glasses.

"Hello, *bonita*!" Claire said as she let herself into Hazel's apartment.

"Hello, future Mrs. Chance Dewdling!" Hazel met her with a glass of Merlot.

"This is just what Tuesday needs." Claire was smiling, and Hazel guessed it was from her use of her future married name. She'd done it on purpose. She'd wanted Claire to know that she supported her.

Claire took a sip. "You're casual," she said, pointing to Hazel's jeans.

"I think I'm going to be dating psychos and weirdos for the long haul, I've got to be able to run fast at a moment's notice." Hazel clinked her glass against Claire's, and they made their way over to the couch.

They bitched about a few new rules implemented at work and talked about an upcoming function before they finished their pre-drinking drinks.

Claire seemed itchy to get going, even though they would be early, so Hazel put on her jacket and followed Claire out of the apartment.

Of course Scott was in the elevator.

"Ladies." He grinned and moved to the back to allow them on. He was holding a full laundry basket.

"You're doing a lot of laundry lately," Hazel noted.

"I don't have anyone to do it for me." He shrugged.

He was hinting at the fact that he used to bring his laundry to her place and they would have "laundry sexathons."

They used to try to bang out one good session during the wash cycle and two slow ones during the dryer cycle.

She knew she was blushing.

"Well, your dirty laundry smells like a pig took a dump in it." Claire waved a hand in front of her face, and Hazel busted out laughing because it was so unexpected.

The elevator opened up to let the ladies off in the lobby, and Scott continued down to the laundry facilities looking far less cocky.

Claire had some advice. "Don't let that fuck boy fluster you. All he cares about is who's petting his dick. And that shouldn't be you anymore. Even if he wants it that way."

They flagged down a taxi as Hazel recovered from her run-in with Scott. It was annoying how quickly he could get to her.

XOXOXOXO

When they were dropped off in front of the theater, they

were clearly too early. After a text from Claire, Chance was at the front door, admitting them both to the building.

Hazel looked all around while Claire and Chance made out. Wolf walked across the lobby doing some sort of busy owner stuff, for sure, and they locked eyes. She felt a chill down her spine. His face did such pleasant things to her body. And it was as if he could tell. He looked her up and down and shook his head.

Was he disappointed? Maybe. But Hazel was sick of mixed messages.

Claire pulled herself from Chance and took them both by the arm. "Let's talk wedding venue. What do you think, Hazel? You're the maid of honor."

Hazel tried to avoid wondering if Wolf was looking at her. "It's certainly pretty."

Chance said, "I spoke to the owners and they said they often rent it out for weddings. If Wolf lets us, we just have to pay for a caterer."

Hazel offered, "Well, that's a great deal. Everyone loves to SAVE MONEY!" She leaned toward where she'd seen Wolf last and shouted the last part.

Claire laughed and patted Hazel on the arm. "It's going to be okay, honey. Chance says that Wolf set up a great date for you tonight."

"Did he? I hope tonight's date isn't related to the last date." She gave Wolf a wide-eyed, accusing stare as he walked back into the lobby.

Wolf ignored her and approached Chance with a wide smile. He had little hints of a dimple. *Jesus.*

"Fine with me, brother. You know—anything you need."

Wolf actually stood right in front of Hazel, blocking her from the conversation.

She turned away and put her back to his as well. There was a crowd starting to form outside. It seemed like a million years ago she was on the other side of that situation.

Wolf put his arm around her, startling her. "Well, pain in the ass, I found the perfect guy for you."

She turned and looked in his face, at his lips. God she wanted to kiss him so much.

"Did you now?"

She was sure in that second that he was going to say it was him. It was inevitable. As annoyed as she was at him, it was like her soul already knew his. They were puzzle pieces clicking into place. They would make the perfect picture.

She felt the loss of the people behind her—Chance and Claire had stepped away to look at another part of the venue.

She wet her lips.

He stuttered then. The confident act he'd put on not two minutes earlier was falling away. She felt him mess with her hair a little.

She angled her body toward his. Her left breast was pressed against his chest now.

His blue eyes were almost glazed over—as if being this close to her was a drug for him.

He took his arm off her shoulders and ran both hands through his hair. He didn't bother to finish the conversation he'd started with her, just walked away like he had an appointment he'd forgotten about.

Hazel felt the rejection slice through her. How could she always be wrong about guys? She was about to leave when one of the Booty Camp employees approached her.

"Hazel? I've got your spot all set up over here. I know Mr. Saber is excited for you to meet your match. His name is Gregory Vander, and it's going to be a great night for you. A hundred and ten percent guaranteed."

So that's how it was. Great. She would meet this Vander person and get him out of the way ASAP. Another date closer to her money back.

The Booty Camp staffer led her to one of the many tables set up in the lobby. The table had a white paper tablecloth and two place settings. There were a few LED candles, the staffer explaining that they weren't allowed to have real flames in the venue.

Hazel pulled out her phone and started liking pictures of her friends on social media to pass the time.

This session was different because some customers were being pulled out of the group and seated at tables like Hazel. The rest were led into the theater seats to hear Chance's spiel. Hazel waved to Claire, who followed the crowd to hear more from Chance.

A Booty Camp staffer came by with a decorated box and set it next to the LED candles. "Please put your cell in here so everyone can concentrate on the person in front of them."

Hazel frowned with the reprimand, but followed the directions. Gregory Vander arrived late but with a big grin. He popped his cell phone in the box and extended a hand like he was normal.

He wasn't bad looking—a little older than she would have liked, but okay.

He took off his ball cap and ran his hand through his hair

so it would fall in its natural style. Which upon closer inspection could only be described as "Dutch little boy on a paint can."

Hazel listened to the Booty Camp girl describe how they would pass out Sharpie markers for the daters, who weren't to talk, but use the table paper to write their questions to each other. They were allowed to use charades-like body language to help their date understand any answers better, if they chose.

Hazel was handed a hot pink one and Vander was handed a bright blue one. Hazel rolled her eyes at the gender-specific colors. The world was moving past these kinds of things nowadays.

Gregory started right in.

Hey, call me Greg. Want to switch markers? Change it up? Fight the system?

Hazel smiled before taking the marker he offered her and handing him hers.

She responded in blue.

Thanks! I love blue. My name is Hazel.

Greg uncapped the pink marker.

You're looking to have a nice date with a guy who isn't creepy, I'm guessing.

Are you psychic? I'm looking to get my money back from this place.

The fine print says I need to go on five dates.

She drew a frowny face.
Greg drew a matching frowny face.

I'm sorry to hear that. Do you want me to write your request on the owner's face in this marker?

Hazel nodded.

That would be fun, but I'm sure you would rather find a nice person to go out with than go to jail.

Greg laughed.

True.

Hazel liked how his eyes sparkled when he was happy, but not enough to feel remotely attracted to the older man.
He wrote some more.

So are they not good at setting up dates?

Not for me. The first guy was escorted out for being offensive and granted a refund. You're the second.

I'm sorry that was your experience. Wow. If you're not into this they should give you your money back. It's almost sexist that he got to leave and you have to stay. They're probably keeping you here as bait because you're so pretty. Did you sign any photo releases? Because they might try and use you in their commercials.

Hazel lifted an eyebrow. Greg's haircut was an issue. But hair could be styled. He was kind of nice.

She watched Wolf walk through the lobby, obviously checking on the dates. When he saw her, he gave her a nod. A self-righteous nod.

Hazel broke eye contact and responded to Greg.

What keeps you busy during the day?

Greg shook his head.

Enough about me. Tell me about you.

Hazel thought it was an odd response because he hadn't said anything about himself, so how could it be too much already?

I'm a teacher. I love my job.

Greg visibly stiffened and then appeared to force himself to relax.

Nice. Where?

Garville Elementary.

Oh. I hear that's a nice place.

It's great. Wonderful staff, kids are cute.

The Booty Camp staff interrupted the quiet dates by clapping.

"Okay. We're going to have the person who arrived last at each table come up here for a moment." She gestured to a large table that was set up in the middle of the lobby. Obviously they'd been working on it during the date period. "That person is going to use these magazine clippings to make a collage they think their date will enjoy based on the information they've gathered during the interactive tablecloth exercise."

Greg stood up and Hazel turned her head in his direction. Her face was crotch level—Greg was fairly tall.

Holy Crap.

He had on the tightest pants she'd ever seen. And not in a rock star way. In a "I bought these grape stranglers twenty years ago and they're turning my testicles into an impressive moose knuckle" way.

Hazel looked down at the table quickly.

Greg patted her shoulder. "I'll be right back."

His voice had a screechy quality that was akin to nails on a chalkboard. Which was an active job hazard for Hazel.

He walked to the center of the room, and sure enough, his pants were so tight that his ass was eating the seam hard.

Hazel leaned forward, put an elbow on the table, and held her fist against her lips.

He couldn't possibly be wearing those pants in public. They were a good two inches too short, as well.

Claire nipped out of the screen room of the theater and waved at Hazel. Her face dropped when she saw Hazel in her thinking pose. She hurried over and sat in Greg's chair.

"What's wrong?" Claire whispered.

"Oh my God. Do you see my date? Look over at that table of people. I bet you can tell by just looking at his back." Hazel pointed her thumb in Greg's direction.

"Holy shit. I recognize that crack. And that Dutch boy haircut. That can't be? Is that Victor Flushlaps?"

Claire got up and circled the table of adults gluing things to poster boards like she was gawking at a car accident before rushing back to Hazel's table.

"That's ol' Flushlaps. Don't you recognize him?" Claire slapped the table with her palm.

The last name sounded familiar. "A little. Do we know him? They said his name was Greg Vander."

"I swear, you never pay attention to the school gossip." Claire lowered her voice. "That's Flushlaps for sure. He has six kids in our school. He's the one we keep catching recording the young teachers instead of his kids at the assemblies. Remember?"

And then Hazel did. Why a married man with six kids would be at an expensive dating service was a mystery. She was always so busy with her kids at assemblies that she never really paid anyone any attention.

"He's the one we think keeps knocking up his wife so he

doesn't have to go back to work." Claire whispered, "Here he comes."

Flushlaps approached the table with his glued masterpiece. And then he saw Claire. He stopped in his tracks.

Claire stood. "Mr. Flushlaps. I think you obviously have to leave Hazel alone at this point."

Wolf came to stand next to Claire. "What's going on?"

Claire pointed in Flushlaps' direction. "I recognize Mr. Flushlaps as a married parent from our school. It's not appropriate for Hazel to be swindled into this match."

Hazel, Claire, and Wolf all seemed to do the same thing at the same moment. They looked at Flushlaps' left hand. There was an obvious divot where he had recently removed a ring from his fourth finger.

Wolf looked harder at Flushlaps. "Wait a minute. You aren't the guy from the picture. I set Hazel up with a different guy. Where's Vander?" Wolf pointed around the room as if he was looking for someone.

Flushlaps cleared his throat and handed Hazel his collage. "Um. I sent in a picture that wasn't me."

Wolf stepped closer. "I was just coming here to tell Mr. Vander that his check bounced. But that would make sense, wouldn't it? Because there is no such animal."

Flushlaps grabbed his phone. Then he backed away from Hazel's table and put up his hands to ward off Wolf.

Chance appeared out of nowhere, but Hazel noticed there was a hush on the crowd. Wolf was mad. He wasn't yelling, but his tone of voice carried distinct authority.

Chance and another Booty Camp staff member came up

on either side of Mr. Flushlaps.

"You don't have to touch me. I'll see myself out."

Claire didn't add any fuel to the flames, but her disapproving assistant principal glare was in full effect.

Hazel slouched in her seat and covered her eyes. This was the second time her date had been kicked out of the venue.

She looked at the collage on her table, its glue still wet. He'd done a good job, Flushlaps/Vander. It had kittens and music and dancing. All things she liked.

Chance came back and set a more relaxed tone, checking in with all the tables to make sure that they were pleased with their experience.

Claire sat in the empty chair, her insta-happiness sparkling on her left hand. As much as Hazel loved her best friend, it was really hard to see her looking all swoony and in love when she was literally getting teabagged with fate's nuts at every turn.

Wolf approached the table with a glass of wine in one hand and some kind of liquor in the other just as she told Claire, "Look at all these people with normal dates."

"Claire, can I sit with her for a few minutes?"

Claire gave Hazel a hopeful glance that included wiggling eyebrows. "Sure. If Hazel doesn't mind."

Hazel nodded once at her friend. She'd rather spend a few minutes with Wolf than wallow in yet another success story. She would let herself be bitter for a few minutes.

Wolf set the glass of wine in front of her, resting it on Flushlaps' masterpiece.

She drained it before he was even completely settled in the opposite chair.

"Whoa. Thirsty?" He took a sip from his glass. The leather bracelets that wrapped around his wrist peeked out from under the blazer he wore over his Booty Camp T-shirt. A dark-wash, slightly beat-up pair of jeans was as fancy as he got.

"No," Hazel replied.

A Booty Camp staff member removed her empty glass and placed a fresh one in front of her.

Hazel ran her finger along its edge and refused to look at Wolf.

After he took another sip of his drink, he gave her some comforting advice. "And that's why checks are so untrustworthy."

"Really? That's what you take from this?" She gave him a hard look.

"Well, his check *did* bounce." Wolf took another swallow.

"I wish I had more middle fingers to give you." Hazel held up the two she had.

He set down his drink and covered her offensive fingers with his hands. "I bet you do. Just pointing out that this attitude might be why we're having issues."

"Not your lack of an actual talent, then? And what about my safety?" She was sick of storming out and letting him enjoy the peace of her absence. "You know what? I've paid for a date, and you've delivered me a possible felon and a definitely married dude with squished balls. I think that qualifies me for a refund. Maybe even some interest. You should hear my rates."

"Are you so sure you weren't with the ex the last couple of days?" He finished his drink and held up his empty glass while making eye contact with her. A staff member took the cue and rushed to the open bar.

"If that was your business, you'd know." She swallowed more of her wine. He was driving her to drink. Because despite their sparring words, there was this thing between them. It was like an unlit fire.

Chance showed up at their table and handed Hazel another drink while holding Wolf's empty. He deftly switched out the white paper. The one with Flushlaps and Hazel's conversation was crinkled into a noisy ball and a fresh one was placed on the table.

"You two should start with the first exercise. I think you might suck at talking. Try writing." He set the markers back down on the table and rearranged the LED candles, as well.

A girl returned with Wolf's drink, and Claire appeared with a fresh wine for Hazel, even though she still had half a glass.

She gave Claire a suspicious look, and her best friend paused to lean down and kiss the top of her head.

Chance offered some advice. "This is quiet date. Your yapping is distracting."

Wolf took the drink. "The security team is taking a hit while Peter is gone. We need to stay on top of this stuff."

"True. I'll look into it. Meanwhile, set a good example, Chief." Chance patted the table before leaving.

Hazel took the blue marker and drew an upside-down middle finger with an arrow pointing at him. Then she added her thoughts.

You suck

He leaned over and plucked the blue marker from her hand.

You're eloquent. I thought you were a teacher.

His handwriting was sloppy, but she could read it.
She took her time with the pink marker and used dots and dashes to spell out his first name. Then she jotted next to it.

Here, practice so your handwriting looks better than a caveman's.

He read it and nailed her with a look that almost had a smile in it.

Did you spend the night with the Ken doll?

She read it and shrugged her shoulders in pretend confusion.

What?

He added to his note.

Your ex. I call him the Ken doll.

Hazel mouthed the word, "*Oh,*" as it became clear to her.

You have a special nickname for my ex. Awesome. And creepy. And not that it matters, but he followed me to my apartment and then I closed the door in his face.

He responded.

Good.

Hazel regarded him for a moment.

Really? It would be so much easier for you if I broke the rules and you got to keep my money and stop me from hassling you.

Maybe. But his energy is all wrong for you.

So the married catfish is a better match?

The guy in the picture he sent in would have been a great match.

Hazel set her marker down and drank her wine.

The atmosphere didn't really invite conversation, but it did allow for extended eye contact.

She held his attention as she tried to figure him out. Was he just a money hungry douche? Pity kiss had been a nice gesture, if not a reassuring one for her womanhood.

He broke first.

What are you thinking about?

I'm trying to figure out what your deal is.

Come up with any answers?

The room was filled with the furious scratching of Sharpies on paper. Hazel noticed that some couples had flipped their paper over to get more writing space. It was a corny exercise, but it was a good trick. It was intimate without having to touch.

I wonder if you even like your job. You seem pretty grumpy.

He rolled his eyes before adding his words near hers.

I'm only grumpy around thickheaded women named Hazel.

That's pretty specific.

I know. Imagine my surprise when you came through the door.

She took another sip of her wine.

Tell me about your tattoo.

Hazel wanted to see if he could hold a normal conversation or if he would continue to be an asshole to her no matter what.

She watched as he lifted the sleeve of his blazer to touch the tattoo she'd been thinking of.

He slowly put his answer on paper.

It's in honor of my sister.

Hazel was taken aback. An actual answer. A sad answer.

She's passed?

He nodded.

It's beautiful. I bet she meant a lot to you.

It was gorgeous ink. An almost abstract version of a dragon—very colorful.

She meant everything.

Hazel ran her fingers over the words. It seemed artificial to make him write them, so she risked a whisper. "I'm sorry you lost her."

Wolf looked away briefly.

He set down his pen and leaned closer, also risking a whisper. "Tell me about the kids in your class."

The smile hit her face before she remembered to be angry with him. She loved her kids. Sometimes people were jerks about the kids she taught. In her experience, the sheltered people of the world couldn't imagine life loving a special-needs individual. But if this guy had anything negative to say about her kids, she would toss her wine at him and then kick him in the balls.

Wolf gave her a confused look. "What? Are they in the Witness Protection Program or something?"

Hazel narrowed her eyes. "They're just really important to me. And I'm super protective of them."

She fished her cell phone out of the box, and Wolf leaned forward to block her illegal usage of the device from the prying eyes around them.

She punched in her code to unlock it and then accessed her pictures. She turned the phone to him and watched his face as he viewed the class snapshot she had taken a few days earlier.

In that picture, she saw their achievements, personalities, and exquisite souls. Wolf swallowed twice before taking the chance to swipe through her other pictures. She went to grab the phone, but he leaned back just enough so that she couldn't reach.

As he swiped, she recalled each picture... Kenzie... Jonah... picture after picture would be flying by of the kids in moments she'd wanted to capture. Kenzie putting together a bird puzzle. Jonah hitting the yes on his conversation board. She checked his face again. If he had any cruel comments, she'd be headed to jail soon.

He flipped the phone around to her when he got to the picture of Scott she'd left on her phone in a moment of weakness.

She took the phone and locked it before putting it back in the decorated box.

"You deserve a real match. Not a guy who's lewd. Not a guy who's actually not the guy he says he is. You need a man."

Wolf hit her with a look that seemed to hold sincere

respect. She was lucky she was sitting because it was a lot to be appraised by him in that way. She rubbed the back of her neck as the hair there stood on end.

He was a powerful energy on his own.

She rubbed her index finger over her bottom lip. The image of him between her legs came like a thunderbolt to her dirty imagination. The pull toward this guy was unlike anything else she'd ever felt. If she had balls they would be blue. Her lady balls were blue.

With everything in her heart and her vagina, Hazel wanted him to say he was her match even though she knew her head would not agree.

Wolf stood. "Grab your phone." He held out his hand to her.

She regarded him for a few seconds before doing what he asked and taking his hand.

He led her back to his office and put her in the center of the room before closing the door.

Hazel turned to face him as he locked it.

Oh shit.

ShE

The first thing he needed to remember was that he was at work. With all his employees outside. And he had a firm rule about getting involved with clients. It wasn't going to happen.

He faced her, and her soft hair and surprised expression triggered him. He stood on his moral ground for a good five seconds, rubbing his fist on the inside of his palm. He leaned over and ran his palms down his thighs to his knees.

He just knew they would fit together.

He looked at her again and she had the very edge of her bottom lip pinned down by her teeth. Pulling his blazer off, he threw it at one of the decorative chairs. It missed and lumped on the floor.

Hazel put the back of her hand on her forehead and let her gaze skim over him. He could hear his blood pumping in his ears and feel it pumping in his dick.

Her tongue peeked out a little as she looked at the fly of his jeans and spoke directly to it like it was a microphone. "I want to make a mistake with you. Right now."

His voice was growly in his own ears when he said,

"You're sure?"

Hazel let her phone fall from her hand and she walked at him like he was a doorway she was going through. At the last second, she put her hand in the center of his chest, backing him against the door he'd just locked.

He gripped the wood behind him with the tips of his fingers. Obviously, reason had it that he wasn't going to sexually indulge in her. But she slid one hand over his chest, up to his face, the other covering the problem he was having below his reason equator.

The loud groan came from him.

Hazel teased him. She held still, her lips just an inch away from his. In a breath she moved closer and skimmed her mouth near his skin, near his jaw.

She pushed up on the tips of her toes and placed an almost kiss on his cheekbone.

"How can someone so pretty…"

She ran her hand through his hair before grabbing a fistful of it and tugging. "…Be so mean?"

Oh God, he could do so much magnificent damage with her.

She gently bit his bottom lip and let her tongue touch it lightly before speaking into his mouth. "Maybe I can learn from my mistakes tonight?"

He licked his own lips and tasted her wine there. And he snapped. He let go of the door and pulled her hard against his chest. This wasn't a kiss that defended her honor, it was simply what the man in him needed.

It was like Pop Rocks, soda, and fireworks in his mouth when he kissed the living hell out of this girl. She might

DEBRA ANASTASIA

irritate him, but her mouth had to be the most fuckable place on the planet. His brain gave him a flash of what her breasts and pussy might look like, and his testosterone hit him in the sex drive like a battering ram.

His hands were all over her, groping tightly—painfully, even—feeling all of her. Maybe even bruising her a little bit. He appreciated the curve of her hip, the pliant firm swell of her ass.

Hazel tilted her head back, her hair tickling his arms as she sighed like his touch was it's own orgasm. His balls felt like they were crying and clapping at the same time.

While he had two handfuls of her generous tits, she retaliated with a demanding grip on his dick. When they locked gazes, the look in her eyes was pure sin. He'd never been regarded with such confident hunger before.

Wolf watched as her hands disappeared under his shirt, pulling it over his head. He felt a happy smile tug on his lips when she ran her hands over his chest and said, "Thank God. This chest hair. Sweet Jesus. I missed these tattoos." Hazel stopped and put her cheek against his chest.

He offered, "I've got hair other places, too."

She covered his mouth with her hand. "Shh. Don't speak. Just be pretty. And do the rough, grabby things. That way I'll hate myself less for demanding that you screw my brains out on that old desk."

The way she took her shirt off was fascinating to watch. It was like she was creating a surrender flag for her inhibitions. This beautiful girl, who had decided he was a mistake she was willing to make, took off her bra in his office. If her boobs felt great before, they looked spectacular now.

She backed away from him and sat on the edge of his desk. "So? Am I a good mistake for you?" She grabbed her nipples.

His mouth went dry. Somewhere in his brain, there was a voice whispering this was a bad idea. A trick, even. But his dick was screaming so loud, and his dick was right about everything, everywhere, all the time. And his dick would never turn Hazel down like this.

As he advanced on her, he watched the pleasure with a tinge of anticipation on her face and decided he would do every damn thing to keep that look there.

She was a treat. An illicit one, but the allure was overwhelming. The mouth, the breasts, the belly button and the slope below it all made this wrong so very right. Her skin was soft, and as he kissed every bare inch she offered, he realized she smelled amazing.

He pulled her close so her chest was pressed into his and used his other hand to throw everything off his desk, including the light. It tossed interesting shadows around the room, but her magnificent face was highlighted, and that was exactly what he needed. He kissed her while lying her gently back on the desk.

"Hey." She stopped him, and he waited to see what she needed while panting a bit. "Don't be gentle, for fuck's sake."

He stood up and looked at the wall for a second, running his hands down his face.

"Am I too much for you?" she asked.

He heard the hint of self-conscious seeping in. And that was criminal.

He crawled on top of the desk, caging her between his

hands and knees.

"No. My problem is that I want a bed. And maybe some rope and lots of lube and good music and a few things that vibrate in a drawer close by. I want to make you come on my face so hard you think you're dying and this"—he looked around his office—"is none of that."

Hazel's returning bravado made her eyes sparkle. "Surely a man that runs a dating service can be creative when he needs to be?"

His only reply to her dare was to put her nipple in his mouth while massaging between her legs with one hand. With the other he balanced above her perilously on the narrow desk. His knees were close to the edge, hemming her in.

She bucked against his hand and hissed at him. "Get to work, then." She grabbed his face and pulled it back up to her mouth.

Hazel was a fire starter. That they went from writing on a tablecloth like civilized humans to being half-naked in the same building was making him shake a little. In a delicious way.

Wolf hopped off the desk and roughly unbuttoned her jeans. Her panties came down when he removed her pants like they were on fire and he was saving her life.

He went straight between her legs, hooking the nearby office chair with his foot and having a damn seat because he was obviously going to be there until he died.

She gasped when he immediately licked her deeply, curving his tongue. She was silk, and her scent was exactly what the feral part of him loved. The combination of her face, sassy personality, and the enchanting masterpiece he was tasting could inspire a man to write a symphony.

When he looked up, she was grabbing her breasts again, and her head was hanging off the other end of his desk. She was enjoying the hell out of this.

He pulled her hips closer to him and wedged his shoulders lower under her thighs so he could wear her sex like a face mask. He needed oxygen less than he needed her to keep making those noises. Hazel flexed around his finger so hard he wished it were his dick. He added another finger, she seemed close to coming until she gave a groan of disappointment.

"What?"

Hazel propped up on her elbows.

"You're being gentle. Again."

He shook his head at her. "You want it harder? Hang the fuck on."

Wolf stood, kicking the chair away. So much for letting her orgasm build and wash over her. With her knees over his shoulders, he added a third finger and let his pinkie test her ass. He found her clit and began sucking on it, beating it up with his tongue, rolling an internal *R* on the edge over and over to give her a terrific sensation. His hand was instantly wet.

"Yesssss." She arched her back and grabbed the edge of the desk, her knuckles white.

He let his fingers be as furious as his heart was pounding.

"Oh God. Use them all. All the fingers. Don't stop."

Wolf took that as an okay to let his pinkie stiffen and gave Hazel a skilled double stuffing.

She lost her damn composure then—screaming his name, praising all the things on his body, and then just cursing like a sailor. He reached up with the hand that was holding her still and covered her mouth. "Shh. Brazen."

Her eyes rolled in her head. She didn't come pretty. She came like it hurt.

It was the hottest damn thing.

In her release, she pulled her body away from him, her head hanging off the edge of the desk again. She flopped around, and every once in a while a shudder ran through her body as an aftershock did its work.

Hazel started laughing. "Holy shit. Holy shit. *Holy shit.*"

Wolf thought his dick might unzip his pants for him. Seeing this woman come for him blew his goddamned mind. The last half hour of his life was seared into his brain and his balls.

"Come here." She waved a lazy hand at him.

"What?" He was still braced above her, slowly working his fingers as she came down.

"Bring your dick to my mouth. I've always wanted to try it like this."

He pulled his hand out from between her legs, and she got the shivers. He placed a kiss right above her pussy before giving it a lick. She still tasted like everything he needed, and the flavor of her lit the fuse at the end of his dick. This sure as hell wasn't something he was supposed to be doing. But still, he walked around the desk so his crotch was in front of her upside-down face while her body remained on his desk.

She yanked on his jeans. "Drop your pants."

Wolf shoved them over his hips, and his boxer briefs went

along for the ride. He couldn't decide if the view was better from this side of the desk or the side he'd just left.

He grabbed her breasts again, and she was obviously still wildly stimulated because she jerked. He thumbed her nipples.

And then she got started.

Hazel managed to grab his balls with one hand while blowing a thin stream of air along the underside of his shaft.

He was a tall guy, and he was thankful for his long wingspan when he realized he could get to her pussy from this angle.

She was a goddamned genius. Hazel's mouth was attending to his dick, and his hands were free to explore all that was before him. She took her hands from between his legs and grabbed two handfuls of his ass.

He stilled when she took him between her lips. Her mind-blowing, silky lips.

She urged him far deeper into her throat than he ever would have pushed himself.

The angle of her head—basically giving him an upside-down blow job—opened up so much of her throat he was almost all the way in before her gag reflex kicked in. He pulled back and started to apologize when Hazel hauled off and slapped his ass. She guided him to the same place again, still gagging but insisting on taking him there with every thrust.

Once he got the rhythm, she spread her legs even more and rubbed her clit. Pinching her nipple with his free hand took more concentration then he'd ever used. She worked magic between his legs, as well. When he was close, she pushed him away and told him to get on his toes. She pulled him closer and sucked on his goddamned balls, tonguing between them.

And when he was about to blow, the backs of his knees shaking with the strain of staying in the position she'd demanded of him, she lined up his dick between her breasts. Using her hands, and he quickly caught on and helped, they made a beautiful titty and dick sandwich. He orgasmed hard and came all over her stomach.

When he had pulsed his last, he collapsed on the floor next to her as carefully as possible. Her face was flushed red from her head hanging off the desk as long as it had. He had to fight his own wobbly legs and arms to scramble back up and help her sit up.

"Whoa. Head rush."

He laughed and hugged her to his chest, holding her woozy body against him.

MONEY'S WORTH

Hazel was sitting naked on his desk while he hugged her to his chest. He was laughing as the blood rushed back to her neck, and fear slammed into her chest. In all her pleasure, she'd forgotten that the last time a man had made her feel that good, he'd left right after.

Actually, Wolf had done her better than Scott ever had. As she closed her eyes and tried to keep the regrets at bay, she thought about how carefree she'd been with Wolf. It was amazing. Being that naked and aroused was something only a person married to their partner for fifteen years would be comfortable with. She was terrified he was planning on breaking her heart and using her vagina to get there.

"Well, you're a surprise. I'll give you that, Hazel."

She shrugged. There was music playing in the lobby. She looked at her lap. Her stupid heart wanted to cuddle this man until he was hard again and then get it on doggy style on the floor. This man. The one who refused to refund her money. Who set her up on a date after kissing her in the elevator.

Oh my God.

What had she done? The attraction between them had been insane, was insane, but he hadn't done anything different except tell her about his tattoo.

She could hear herself swallow.

Wolf kissed the top of her head and pushed a lock of hair behind her ear. She was too afraid to look at his face.

"Obviously, we can't tell anyone about this." Wolf added a forced laugh.

She looked at the penis she'd just jerked off between her boobs. It was a very nice penis.

We can't tell anyone about this.

That's what he thought. Of course. Because he probably did this all the time. Took a customer into his office for a little "refund" time.

She shoved him away and began the hunt for her clothes.

"Hazel?"

She thought she heard him swallow.

"Don't worry. I won't tell anyone. And as soon as I take a shower and all your jizz is gone, there won't be evidence, either. You'll be free and clear." Her jeans were tangled up with her heels and her panties. They made a puzzle her angry hands had trouble solving.

"That's not what I mean. That was amazing, and you were amazing. But—"

"Yup. I took your finger up my butt. And I liked it. Jesus." She sat in his desk chair while she put on her panties.

"I just shouldn't have done this with you. It's against the rules. And if I don't set you up on a date, the staff will know what happened, and I just want to make sure that I'll have your discretion. "

Hazel covered her mouth and bit her tongue to keep herself from saying anything that would make this worse. She put her jeans back on. Her hands were sticky from his pleasure, which was also on her stomach.

"Hazel."

She shot him a look. He was still naked.

"You haven't even put your dick away and you're already worried about how bad I'll make you look?" She pushed her hair away from her face, looking for her top and bra.

"Hazel."

She found them and put on her shirt before shoving her bra in the back pocket of her jeans. "Stop saying my name like you know me. You don't know me."

He started putting his jeans on. "Don't leave. I can't. Just let me figure this out."

She finally put on her heels. She walked to the office door. Tears started to work on her now, and she didn't want them.

"You can't leave like this."

There was a mirror on the wall, and she could see his reflection as he put his Booty Camp shirt back on. She gave him a second to think of something that would make what they just did more about the connection she felt to him than what happened in their pants.

"I can see your nipples through that shirt. Put your bra on and let me clean up this stuff from my desk.

She shook her head and turned the doorknob.

She got it open about an inch before he came up fast behind her and slammed the door shut.

She turned her head so she could see him out of her peripheral vision.

"Just let me get this together. This is my business here. I have to set an example."

Hazel turned more so she was close to him again. Her traitorous vagina wanted more from him. His mouth, his tongue. Those fingers. But amazingly, her heart was feeling the burn hard. Maybe even worse than after Scott had left her.

"You're letting me leave or I'm screaming." She lifted one eyebrow.

He ran his hand through his hair and then hit his fist against the door. "Fine. I'll walk you out."

"You can't." Hazel hated that a tear fell. She would have paid someone two thousand dollars right then to keep that little bit of dignity inside.

He wiped her tear away with his thumb. She pushed his hand away roughly and managed to backhand the second tear that fell. Then Hazel got on her tiptoes and spoke very close to his lips. "Because I came all over your jeans, Wolf."

He looked down and sure enough, there was a super duper wet spot all over the crotch of his jeans. He cursed, but he left his hand against the door, keeping her trapped.

Hazel needed an out. She was way too close to having the chin-crumpling breakdown she was afraid she was going to have.

"You'll see to it that I have another date. You know what fun I am now, so finding a match for me shouldn't be a problem." She lifted her head and gave him the best fuck-you glare she could.

She watched his face as he realized what she'd said. First disbelief, then hurt, then anger.

"Well, Miss Lavender, you certainly know how to get your money's worth." He stepped back and gave her back her personal space.

Hazel looked at him and unbuttoned the top three buttons on her shirt, giving herself a scandalous neckline. She wanted to launch a parting comeback, but she knew she wouldn't make it through it without her voice cracking.

Instead, she turned and flung open his door. The crowd in the lobby looked instinctively towards the movement.

Hazel tossed her shoulders back, pulled her bra out of her back pocket, and twirled it on the end of her finger like a keychain.

Behind her, she heard Wolf mutter, "Fuck."

She wasn't expecting the slam of the office door or the pounding fists that sounded like he was punishing the door and his knuckles at the same time.

MISTaKES WERE MadE

Hazel regretted the tit show she was putting on, but she was—ironically—too proud to cover up. A Booty Camp staff member opened the front door for her in a hurry. She stood on the sidewalk and took a deep breath.

That was crazy. What a goddamned roller coaster.

Claire was calling her name, and Hazel waved, trying not to cry.

Claire saw through her. "Oh, sweetheart. What happened? You guys looked like you wanted to eat each other."

Her friend went in for a hug, but Hazel took a step backwards. She couldn't let Claire get everything she had on her body and hands smeared on her. They'd been best friends for too long for that bullshit.

"What? Are you hurt?" Claire seemed to piece together the disheveled outfit, the bra dangling from her hand and the—Hazel could only imagine—sex-messed hair. "Oh, you weren't hurt physically."

Hazel shook her head.

"Do you need me or do you need space?"

Hazel loved how Claire cut to the chase.

Hazel held up two fingers.

Claire got it. "The second one? Okay. I get it. Let me hail you a cab. Put your bra away and button your top. Where's your purse?"

Hazel pointed at the theater doors.

"Back there?" Claire texted someone, probably Chance, while Hazel did as she was told, tucking the bra in her pocket and fastening her buttons.

She thought of Wolf's parting words. And how worried he was about his business.

Chance was trotting down the stairs with her purse in hand and Wolf hot on his heels.

"Everything okay?" Chance was a huge dude, but he was good at reading people, it seemed.

Wolf slowed down next to her, glowering.

Hazel rarely told anyone she'd been interested in acting for a while, that she'd been in a few plays in high school and two in college. Of course Claire knew, but she would never rat out her friend.

So Hazel put her acting skills to work. She pointed at Wolf just as a few more Booty Camp staff members trickled onto the stairs.

"I made a pass at him. He refused me. He owes me something, and I want my thousand dollars' worth. But he turned me down. And I'm pissed." Hazel watched the knowledge of what she was saying reach his face. Confusion, then relief, and then... and then she couldn't tell what he was thinking because her vision was blurry. "So, you better get my money back soon, Wolf."

Wolf nodded once and looked at his feet.

The cab driver honked, clearly not interested in their drama.

She settled in the backseat as Chance handed her purse to her. Wolf pushed his way past his friend and held out her phone. She took it without touching his fingers.

"I'm sorry I hurt you."

His gruff whisper got to her. Hazel was pissed, but she wasn't about to ruin the man's life. She turned her head to avoid looking at him and instead watched the reflection of the scene in the back passenger window. Claire pulled Wolf out of the way.

"I'm texting you already. Let me know when you're ready for ice cream."

Hazel put her hand near her eye again. Claire knew Hazel was on the edge and slammed the door closed, slapping the side of the cab to let the driver know it was clear for takeoff.

XOXOXOXO

Claire was in Wolf's face before the cab had even turned the corner. "Let's go have a discussion, okay?"

She sounded pleasant, but her face had a mama bear quality to it. Chance put his arm around Claire and led her back inside.

Wolf didn't want anyone in his office until it stopped smelling like a newlyweds' hotel room. But Claire didn't give him any choice as she entered before he did.

He stepped around her and Chance, closed the door behind them, and began cleaning up the disarray.

"Wow. You really had to fight my girl Hazel off, huh?

Knocked the damn lamp over? And wet your pants?" Claire was far too shrewd for bullshit.

Wolf shook his head. "That's not how it went down."

"No, I didn't think so. I've got to tell you, she loved that last nut-dropping. She trusted the dick bag. She let him into her world. And being loved by her? Let me tell you a secret—it's life altering. She's the most caring, funny, sexy as fuck woman I have ever met. And you know it. I can see it in your face."

Wolf knelt down to gather the pictures from the floor while Chance righted the lamp.

"She's never, in all the damn years I've known her, dragged a guy into an office and forced herself on him. Never."

Wolf stood with the folder and set it on his desk again. "It wasn't like that."

"I know." Claire bent down and grabbed a wayward picture from the floor. She spun it to face him. It was Hazel. "I made her do this; did you know that? I made her do this with me so we could laugh together. Have fun. I never imagined how goddamned intense it is. That I would meet him..." She trailed off and touched Chance's face.

"But *you* know that it's intense. That for some reason, this place has success despite the awful name." She pointed to the logo on Chance's shirt. An upside-down heart wearing a thong.

"I brought her here broken, and you've been a shit to her. And maybe that's your curse. You're allowed to make other people happy while you stew in your own miserable juices, but you can't drag her down with you. I won't let you take her." Claire was pointing at him.

Wolf sat behind his desk and held his head. He wanted to feel regret about all of it. Remind himself of the mistake he made. A lapse in judgment. Here, in his rented office with his best friend and her best friend, his brain wouldn't stop.

A slideshow of mental snapshots he'd taken during his time with her was on a constant loop in his imagination. And it was magnificent.

He'd fucked up. Clearly. He'd hurt her. She wanted it hard, but not torturous—emotionally, anyway.

And Claire was right. Hazel was broken. Someone had taken the breath-taking energy that allowed her to care for a roomful of kids like his sister as not just a passion but a profession and ground cigarette butts in it.

And then he made it worse. Instead of letting that incredible orgasm session make her feel stronger, he'd made her feel cheap.

Claire was still railing at him. He had to go and dry his jeans with the hand dryer in the bathroom. He had to go buy her flowers and chocolate and get a boom box to hold up under Hazel's window.

Chance might not have his "gift" of making matches, but he'd been in the game so long he knew the signs of good chemistry. He'd been impressed with Chance's strong decision-making skills in the past. Chance wanted the redhead in front of him, so he'd handled it so she wasn't a client. Done.

Wolf didn't know how to do that without being creepy. He also knew that any relationship he got tangled in was doomed. His mother and grandmother had drilled that much into his head. And Hazel deserved to not have her heart get flushed down the drain again.

Wolf stood up. "It's better for her to not let me get attached to her. I'm doomed, see? Ask him. He'll tell you."

He walked out of his office, ignoring the sneaky glances from his nosy staff. Wolf prided himself on being a constant. They never saw him lose control. They could trust him enough to follow his ass around the country, helping with this elaborate dating service.

He pushed the door to the men's room out of the way and stood in front of the hot blow dryer for a few minutes before he realized that he should take his pants off and hold them under in order for them to dry quicker.

He did just that. While he held the denim under the blower, he gently punched the tile. He'd made a fool of her. And he was seriously pissed. He couldn't have taken a second to tell her she was the most beautiful woman in the world? That his heart was nearly on fire when she was in the room? No, he'd wanted to cover his ass first. Like that mattered more than reaffirming the sexuality she'd displayed with him.

He knew that wrapping her up, dragging her away, and keeping her for himself was what he wanted, of course, but it scared him to think he could be the next pain in her life. Wolf was also scared of the pain he would feel if he faced how incredible she was. And that was pretty fucking selfish. Christ, he was so full of his damn self.

When the jeans were done drying, he slipped them back on and almost burned his dick when the metal of his zipper was four thousand degrees from the heat of the dryer. He pulled the material away until he could tolerate the heat. Then he went to the sink to wash her off of him. He wasn't even ashamed when he smelled his hands again before contaminating the perfection of her on his skin with soap and water. He washed his face, as well.

He grabbed a paper towel and was patting his face dry when Chance came in behind him.

"So, that happened." Chance went to the urinal to handle his business.

Wolf tossed the towel in the trashcan. "It did."

"Hazel's got you screwed up in the head, huh?" Chance shook off and tucked himself away before going to the same sink Wolf had just used.

"Why do you say that?" Wolf felt his eyebrows knit together.

"Because you look like you were just run over with a truck driven by a vagina." Chance went to the hand dryer and stuck his big, meaty mitts under the air stream.

Wolf almost chuckled. "Yeah. You know how that works out for me. No strings. No feelings. That's what I do."

Chance opened the men's room door and held it for Wolf. "Not this time. In case you haven't noticed."

Wolf walked back into the lobby and started checking on tables and matches, staying out in the open far longer than he normally did.

He was trying to keep himself from going to her apartment building and finishing what they'd started.

Him

Hazel was done. She was done with boys. Done with men. Her vagina was retiring. Her heart had tendered its registration without the benefit of two weeks notice. She'd known this man for barely any time. He wasn't allowed to affect her like this.

Hazel stepped into the hot shower and took care of the business of washing him from her body. She blushed as she thought of the way she'd been with him. How dare he be an ass when she had finally gotten in touch with a sexual version of herself she was so proud of.

She washed her hair three times. When she was done and toweled off, she wrapped herself in her pink satin robe. It was ice cream time.

She had some in the freezer since Scott had pulled out of her body and her life. It had freezer burn, but it would do. She got a spoon and the container and sat on the couch.

Hazel hated how typical she was being, committing so many stereotypical stereotypes. But she deserved it. This was the second orgasm induced by the opposite sex in six months that ended in her crying.

Her phone kept dinging with updates from Claire. She kept her friend at bay, promising she was okay and just needed space. She also told Claire to enjoy her time with Chance. Lord knew what the future held for those crazy kids. They might get married in a few weeks and then have to deal with an extended time apart while he helped stupid Wolf with his stupid business.

She realized she was looking at a blank TV screen. Hazel set the ice cream on her coffee table and noted that the remote was too far to reach without getting up. Instead, she leaned back into the deep cushions of her couch.

And the scenes she'd just washed from her body came back almost as hard as she had earlier.

His fingers. His chest. Knowing that she had given him a completely raw version of herself. She'd been daring.

And she had only herself to blame. One kind look of respect and she was in his office with her bra on the floor.

Maybe she'd been too forward. Was the lack of Scott driving her to do stupid things? Obviously getting naked with the guy she'd been mostly fighting with should not be a proud moment. But she'd had trouble finding shame when his lips had been on hers. Either set.

She texted Claire again that she was okay and planning on turning in.

Hazel didn't want to go to bed, so she stretched out on the couch in her robe. The beauty of living alone. The word "alone" echoed in her head as she closed her eyes.

The knocking on her door was incessant. It took her a few minutes to realize it wasn't part of her dream. It was really happening. She looked out the window; it was still dark. Clicking her phone to life, she saw that it was 2:30 a.m. Hazel grabbed a large statue of a horse from the end table by the couch for a weapon and stood. It had to be somebody from within the building. She hadn't buzzed anyone through the front door.

She startled when the knock banged again as she tried to peek through the peep hole.

Finally she asked, "Who the hell is it?"

Maybe there was a malfunction in the fire alarm or something, but she'd lived too long in the city to throw her door open without knowing who was on the other side.

"The big bad Wolf." He looked right into the peep hole.

She looked down and fastened her robe when she realized she hadn't even put on her pajamas.

"Not by the hair of my chinny chin chin," she responded from somewhere deep in her casual, weird-knowledge brain storage.

She watched as he sighed. "That's original. I've never heard that before ever."

Hazel didn't say anything.

Finally he replied, "I'll huff, and I'll puff, and I'll blow your house in," while dragging his knuckle down the door's surface. She set down the horse.

She was angry but she didn't need a weapon to handle him.

He fanned out a bunch of hundreds where she could see them. "I want to refund your money."

She was shocked, and her heart fell at the sight of the cash. His refunding her money communicated the conclusion of the fine print version of their deal, so he wouldn't see her anymore.

Hazel didn't want to end it. But she knew he was just as bad as Scott, sniffing around when his balls grew cold.

She unlatched the door and opened it.

"You're not wearing anything?"

"You're not getting any. So don't ask." Hazel held her hand out for the money. "I hope my interest is in here." She gave him the coldest look she could muster without letting the heat her body was experiencing at his nearness interfere.

He handed her the cash. "It's not."

"Great." She started to close the door.

He put his hand out to stop her. "I also wanted to deliver an apology. I was..."

"An asshole? A fuckhead? A selfish prick?"

"Unprepared for how hot that whole scene got." He jammed his hands in his jeans.

"I'm glad it worked for you. Do I owe you money for *your* services, then?" She tossed the cash at his face. She guessed he wasn't even close to who her imagination had painted him to be.

Anger made his jaw twitch. He stuck his foot out when she tried to close the door for the second time.

"Hazel, I just wanted to talk about it."

"Okay. What's there to say?" Hazel grabbed at her robe, which was failing to stay secure, being silk and all.

"I keep putting my foot in my mouth. I wanted to say it was great, you were amazing. I can't be involved with customers, but if I could, I would pick you." He left the money on the hallway floor.

"So, if tonight wasn't involved for you, I wonder what is?" Hazel stepped backwards to give herself space from his excuses.

He stepped in and let the door close behind him. "It was involved, very involved. I can't stop thinking about you. And I don't want you mad at me."

"The fact that you think this is me being mad at you as opposed to you apologizing for your mistake tells me a lot." Hazel touched the horse sculpture on the end table thinking about holding it to ward him off.

"Are you afraid of me?" He held up his hands after noticing her reaching for the heavy horse. "For that, I'm sorry. I'll leave right now. You were just so fierce it never occurred to me that I would intimidate you." He reached behind him for the doorknob.

"Don't act like the good guy right now." Hazel lifted the statue and hugged it to her chest.

He opened the door again, and she set the horse back down. He knelt to pick up the money for her. This time when he held it out, she took it.

"You can still go on the dates if you want. I'll make sure it's all on the up and up. We like the customer to be satisfied." He seemed to regret the words the minute they left his lips.

She left the obvious unsaid. He was so goddamned good-looking. The messy hair he hadn't bothered to fix. The eyes that seemed to have a bit of the canine wolf in them when he looked at her. He was trouble.

"Okay. I'm going to go." He stepped backwards.

She set the cash near the horse. Some fell to the floor; it certainly wasn't in a neat pile.

A devilish comment came to her. She bit her lip for a second before delivering the parting shot. "So was this a booty call from Booty Camp?"

Wolf shook his head at her bad joke. He seemed to want to expand on the conversation but hesitated. "So you know, the guy who gets to see you like that—" he gestured at her satin robe and what Hazel could only imagine was really wild hair—"is a lucky goddamned bastard."

She touched the hair on her shoulder. The elevator sounded behind him, and Hazel made a confused face. Two thirty or so in the morning was a super weird time for the elevator to be hitting her floor. Scott used to call the third floor "the nursing home." A lot of her neighbors were retired.

And speak of the devil—Scott stepped out of the elevator. Well, stepped was being kind. He was blasted. He stumbled and sprawled.

"Hazel. You're awake. I needed to feel you." Scott rested an arm against the wall to balance himself.

Wolf looked from Scott to Hazel and back again. "Good night, then." He turned and stalked back on to the elevator.

Hazel couldn't believe her damn lady garden. It had been hoping for more action the minute it knew Wolf was in the building, despite all her good sense and heartbreak. It had no chill or loyalty. She slammed the door, knowing that she would hear it from the neighbors on either side for her noisy early morning. She sure as shit wasn't letting a drunk Scott into her apartment.

Leave Her Be

Wolf wasn't in the elevator two seconds before the doors that had just slid closed reopened. He hoped it was her, that she'd come after him to welcome him into her apartment. He'd been a dick. Instead of telling her he was refunding her money so that she wouldn't be a client anymore and he could ask her on a proper date, he'd gotten defensive and offered her another date with a different person.

He couldn't get it right. It was probably because he refused to make a decision and stick to it. Go after her and stay after her until she was his, or let her have a happily ever after that could never come from being with him. Assuming she would even have him.

Instead of Hazel at the mouth of the elevator, her stupid ex-boyfriend came flopping in like a human noodle.

"Hold that door. Wait? Aren't you the guy that was kissing her the other day? I should kick your ass!" Scott went for a weak-wristed punch that Wolf sidestepped. The man punched the elevator wall instead as the doors closed.

"I was. And aren't you the bitch who broke her heart? And you have a girlfriend already?" Wolf couldn't let this guy make himself into a knight in shining armor in his own head. "Well, not anymore. She broke up with me because I called her Hazel when I was balls-deep in her twat." Scott slid to the floor.

Wolf was elated that Hazel had apparently rejected this guy who wanted to feel her. Wolf looked down at Scott. "You're a fucking prince, huh?"

"Hazel loves me. I know I can get back in between the juicy, you know. Tonight, after a few drinks, I had no idea why I left Hazel in the first place. Damn new girl laughs when she pops off her load." Scott shook his head like this was a super disappointing trait. "It was cool at first, but now it's horrible. But Hazel? When I got her off, she would get all pretty pink and scream my name. I miss it. I need to go back up there and talk to her. I love that robe." Scott started climbing up the wall to get back to the buttons on the elevator wall just as they reached the lobby.

Wolf reached over and hit the emergency stop button. It started a loud, incessant, blaring alarm, which was probably a bad move, but Wolf grabbed a fistful of Scott's shirt and shoved him against the wall. "You dumb fuck. If you ever go near Hazel again, I'll knock some fucking sense into you. Do you hear me?"

Scott tried to fight back, but he was useless from alcohol. Wolf was able to collapse Scott's knee by tapping behind it with the heel of his boot.

As Scott went down, Wolf slapped him in a friendly yet painful way. "Stay the fuck away from her."

Wolf hit the button to restart the elevator. Restraining himself from beating up Scott took a lot. He knew there might be a video camera on him right now, and he didn't want to get arrested tonight. But he wasn't opposed to an unrecorded beatdown for this fucking jackhole. No matter what Hazel thought of Wolf, he respected women. And Scott clearly didn't.

Wedding Plans

Hazel didn't see Claire until Monday morning, but they had texted over the weekend.

Hazel was waiting in front of the school for the bus that had a majority of her students on it. It was always good to have a few extra hands to help with unloading Jonah.

Claire also had bus duty in the morning. The two stood close while they waited for the buses to roll in.

"So how are your parents taking the engagement and wedding news?" Hazel wanted to start in with Claire's news so that maybe she could avoid talking about Booty Camp for a while longer.

"Went better than I thought. Mom was, surprisingly, on board. My father's concerned that it's too soon. My sister wants to know if Chance has a brother." Claire laughed and sipped her coffee. Hazel hadn't brought hers out because she needed two free hands when the bus arrived.

"Does he?" Hazel smiled.

"No. The closest person he has besides his dad is..." Claire trailed off.

"His coworker?" Hazel offered.

"Yeah. Which is why Wolf is his best man. Is that going to be okay? We have a dress fitting later this week. Did I tell you yet? It's going to be so fast. It's just you and my sister and Wolf and Peter, the security guy from Booty Camp in the bridal party." Claire looked worried.

"It's fine. Wolf and I spoke on Saturday. It's fine." Hazel tried to be convincing.

"So are you going to tell me what happened in the office? Ever?" Claire wrapped her hands around her coffee.

"You heard it. I tried to seduce him and failed." Hazel didn't make eye contact.

"Okay. Did I tell you we're going to get married in the nude on a hoverboard?" Claire put her hand on Hazel's arm.

"Great. I love that idea. My butt vibrating on top of a new age skateboard is the best idea ever," Hazel responded to Claire's obvious fib.

"Just tell me. I mean I already know. You and Wolf got it on. And you took the blame so he wouldn't look bad." Claire was right—she already knew.

Hazel looked at her boots.

"Chance was really impressed with you. About that whole thing. He went on and on about it." Claire rubbed the center of Hazel's back.

"Wolf gave me my money back."

"He did? Wow. Did he ask for an official date, then?"

Hazel could almost hear her friend coordinating a double wedding in her head. She shot that down with her next statement.

"He sure did. He's going to set me up on a really great date for free if I want. Told me he'll get the match right this time.

And it wouldn't be with him." Hazel finally did look at Claire and saw the anger flare on the redhead's face.

"That dick banana. He is the most clueless man. Does he not see the sparks between you two? Jesus. It's like watching clothed porn when you look at each other."

"He's not the guy for me." Hazel shook her head and saw the bus she was waiting for in the distance.

"If he's hard-headed enough, he'll miss out on that opportunity." Claire set her coffee down on the low retaining wall. She always pitched in if Hazel's bus got there before the rest of the buses. "Tell me what happened in the office."

Hazel shook her head. "You heard what I said about it. When's the dress fitting?"

"This Thursday night at Fancy Pants. Seven sharp." Claire and Hazel stepped forward as the bus threw open its doors.

"I'll be there." Hazel waved at Kenzie, who looked at her through the window for a few seconds before waving back. Hazel noted the progress. She didn't need any man at all when she had smiles like these in her life.

XOXOXOXO

Hazel's week was a busy one. She had two recitals and a bunch of IEP meetings to prepare for, so she didn't get a ton of time to obsess about Wolf. Though she did have to deal with increasingly frequent run-ins with Scott. He'd even had a vaseful of roses delivered to school. Hazel put one rose in each of her coworkers mailboxes to brighten their day. She wasn't going back to Scott. She wasn't letting anyone get close to her again for a long time. So, she had to mentally prepare for the Fancy Pants dress fitting. She didn't even know what the dresses looked like, though she knew they were a pretty melon color.

She had to remember to harden herself in case Wolf was there, too. Claire had warned her that the men were getting their tuxes sized, but she was pretty sure it was in a different section of the bridal store.

After Hazel did paperwork and filled out some observations on Thursday, she headed home.

She ate leftover mac and cheese while looking through her closet. The lies she told herself about what she was going to wear were loud in her ears. The dark jeans and sweater she was four hundred percent *absolutely going to wear* were cast aside.

Hazel wanted to look good. And that was okay. It was a special day for her best friend. It was okay if she put on her long black skirt with the slit up the side with heeled boots and topped it with a matching black top. Her makeup was on point; her favorite perfume was behind her ears and her knees. And maybe she was wearing her favorite sexy undies and bra.

As Hazel was leaving her apartment, she gave a little scream when Scott came up behind her and put his hands on her hips while she was locking her door.

"Jesus!" She whirled on him.

"You look amazing." His hands were still on her hips.

"Let go of me!" Hazel pushed him away.

"I'm sorry! I thought you knew I was here. Where are you headed? Can I come?" He wiggled his eyebrows right after the word *come*.

She noted his innuendo. "Too soon, Scott."

"Again, I'm sorry. I just wanted to make sure the flowers I sent you arrived." Scott stepped out of her way and damn near tripped over himself so he could beat her to the button and call it to the third floor.

"I did. I passed them out to staff." She made a point of not thanking him.

He looked disappointed before recovering. "They work hard just like you. Glad you did that with them."

The elevator doors opened and they both stepped on. "Where you headed?"

Hazel leaned past him and hit the button to take them to the lobby. "I have a dress fitting."

"Really? That's great. You going to see that guy?"

Scott was jealous. And Hazel allowed herself to feel a little bit pleased about that. "Which guy?"

Scott gave her a look like she was a pitcher of water he was filling that was about to overflow. "The one that tried to kill me right here the other night?"

"What?" Hazel was shocked.

"Yeah, we were alone here, and he just attacked me for no reason when I told him I wanted to make it up to you, to get you back." Scott gave her his most earnest look.

"Wolf is... unpredictable." Hazel was grateful that the elevator was opening at the lobby.

Scott stepped out with her. "Just be careful around him, right? I worry about you."

Hazel nodded and headed out. Scott went back to the elevator.

She took off walking, grateful the Metro stop was close to

her apartment because these were not walking heels.

X☉X☉X☉X☉

Fancy Pants was the area's most well-known bridal shop. Despite the silly name, they had a great reputation. Claire had raved about them when she was fitted for a bridesmaid's gown last year. And told her that there was clearly a man's side and woman's side.

Hazel walked out of the Metro stop and spied Fancy Pants lit in white lights and gauzy window displays.

Wolf was there, leaning against an old-looking sports car, and Chance and Claire were cuddled together but obviously talking to Wolf. There was another guy there Hazel didn't recognize. She guessed he was Peter from Booty Camp. She felt her cheeks get warm, knowing he might have witnessed her last departure from the theater.

Wolf was watching her when she looked back at him again. Dark jeans and long sleeves never looked so good. He acknowledged her.

She looked down to make sure she wasn't going to trip on the curb, and when she looked back, he was in conversation again.

Claire detangled herself from Chance and met her halfway, grabbing her in a full-body hug. "They were able to get my dress! We get to try it on right now!"

Claire started jumping, and as was tradition, they jumped together—no matter where they were in the world.

Claire linked arms with Hazel and led her over to the group. "My sister couldn't make the drive, it's too far, so I'll try on her dress. We're the same size, anyway. Peter, this is Hazel. Hazel, Peter."

Peter was hot. Almost as tall as Chance with blazing red hair. If Hazel didn't know better, she would think that Peter was related to Claire. With impeccable cornflower blue eyes and a nice auburn scruff going, he could be on the cover of a magazine. He held out his hand and shook Hazel's.

"Nice to meet you." He gave her a bright grin.

"You sure you're not a member of the bride-to-be's family?"

He touched his hair and mussed it. "All us redheads are from the same clan somewhere."

Hazel started a conversation with Peter because it seemed the least awkward way to get into the store and to the proper side for the dress fitting without dealing with Wolf. "I don't think I saw you at Booty Camp. Claire mentioned you worked there?"

"I'm security. But I had a family emergency, so I didn't get back until today. I doubt I would have missed running into you." Peter winked, and Wolf cleared his throat behind her.

"She's a client, so..."

Hazel finally looked at Wolf. "Am I? I thought I got a refund?"

Wolf clenched his jaw while he grabbed the door from Chance and held it open for Hazel and Peter.

"You got a refund, but you're still a client if you decide to go on a date," Wolf clarified.

Claire waited until Peter had cleared the door before she stepped through, giving Wolf the coldest glare she could manage.

He stepped close behind her and spoke near her ear. "My door's open for you as a client."

His words, whispered so near, started everything in her panties all over again. He was infuriating. She decided right then she would focus all her attention on Peter for the entirety of the wedding events. Including this one.

Hazel stood next to Claire while she explained what was going to happen.

"You guys are going to the Pants side over there." She pointed to the right of the lobby which was filled with flowers and plush chairs for luxurious waiting. "And we will be on the Fancy side. When you're done, you can wait for us here, and afterward we'll be going out for drinks and dancing. Okay? Chance already bought a bottle service here, so you can have a glass of wine after you're out of the clothes."

She kissed Chance like they would be parted for four months instead of forty-five minutes. And after the boys walked away, Claire made Hazel do the jumping again.

"I hope it looks as good as it did in the magazine. I'm so excited. But I think I might puke. Oh my God. You have to FaceTime this for my sister and mother, okay? They don't want to miss anything." Claire squeezed Hazel's hands.

"Of course. No problem. This store has wifi?" Hazel pulled out her phone and saw that she already had an alert offering to join Fancy Pants network.

"Okay. I think let's do you first, and once that's out of the way, I can try on mine." Claire greeted the shop girl as she approached.

"Oh, here's our bride. I've steamed the dress and laid it out in the main dressing room. Would you like a glass of champagne?" To Hazel, she introduced herself as Lottie.

"I think, Lottie, maybe we have to get Claire into her dress before she explodes." Hazel smiled and reached into Claire's purse for her phone.

Claire didn't even try to argue as Hazel changed her plan. Hazel waited until Lottie had taken Claire into the main dressing room, which was along the wall that the Fancy side and the Pants side shared. Hazel overheard Lottie explain to Claire that she had to be careful because the wall was papered to look solid, but it was really a temporary divider that the store had worked into the design.

Hazel tried her best not to think of having to spend an evening on the town with Wolf. But on the other hand, she was really glad she looked good.

THERE SHE IS

Wolf waited on the Pants side of the bridal store while Chance made some last-minute decisions on vest shape. Peter sat in the chair next to Wolf. Peter was a great guy and a reliable employee. Booty Camp was lucky to have him. Right now, Wolf wanted to punch him in the face.

"So, is Hazel a client or isn't she?"

Because he obviously had the same thing on his mind that Wolf did.

"If she's not, I'm going to slip into a dress, bust over there, and ask her out. Did you see that leg? Holy shit. And that rack was not kidding."

Wolf didn't look at Peter but reached out and squeezed his shoulder. "She's a client."

Peter removed Wolf's hand. "Easy, boy. Wow. Sorry to touch your stuff. When'd you get so uptight?"

Chance interrupted. "Wolf's pretending she's not a real girl when I'm pretty sure he's hiding a tattoo of her name on his back."

"Oh." Peter stood up so he was shoulder to shoulder with Chance. "That's how it is. That makes a lot of sense. You got great taste, boss."

Chance shook his head like Wolf was a TV show they were watching. "Our boy is going to fuck this up. Which would be a shame because I'm no matchmaker descendent or anything, but they have chemistry out his dingdong."

Wolf held up his middle finger. "I'm not involved with Hazel. Where are these monkey suits? Do we have to wait for you to get your makeup done first or something?"

"The gentleman is going to take your inseams first, you bastard." Chance pointed to the set of steps where an older man was waiting. "He's going to take your measurements—but don't start crying, he won't measure your dick—and then you have to put on shoes and some samples for him to see how the suit hangs on you. Which you should know by now, Mr. I Own My Own Business."

Wolf didn't even have a real need for a suit. There was an odd wedding or two, but the business was moving too fast for him to worry about the trappings a guy with his annual income usually had to grapple with.

Booty Camp's success had been a steamroller. Luckily, he'd made Chance the recognizable face of the Booty Camp brand. It saved Wolf's anonymity, and Chance loved the limelight.

Chance had been a friend since high school. Ironically, Wolf had stopped a group of assholes from beating up a much smaller Chance in the locker room. He'd inspired loyalty from the younger guy. And Wolf didn't have to worry about him when he graduated because Chance shot up in his junior year and took to weight lifting.

Wolf reached his lowest when he lost Faith. No one had

known what to do to help him move past his sobbing anger at fate. But Chance had recognized that the pain was Wolf's bully and stayed next to him until he could function again.

And that was what he'd needed. Faith's death had been a shock. She'd had a cold that turned into bronchitis that turned into pneumonia. Wolf had already been at odds with his mother and grandmother over the woman he'd been dating at the time. They were positive she was wrong for him, and he married Clarissa anyway.

They thought that he was too young to make permanent choices like that. He worked toward his college degree and in the yard of the local lumber company at the same time. His marriage dissolved.

When he decided to turn the matchmaking skill every female in his family excelled at—and, for some unknown reason, he'd inherited—into a business, he'd made his mom and grandmother very angry.

They felt it was disrespectful. The matchmaking was like religion; it should be practiced as a way to increase the positive energy in the world. No amount of proof he dragged before them would sway their opinion. First, it was the small wins, marriages and pregnancy announcements, and then it was nationwide success with waves of babies being born after Booty Camp blew through a city. Wolf believed it was the best use of what he could do. And sure, it made money, but it also made lots of people very happy. Well, everyone except Hazel.

And he'd taken Chance for that ride with him. Wolf loved his family. Still missed his sister all the time. So he would try not to make this anything but fun for his non-blood brother despite the boner-for-Hazel guilt wrestling that was his new hobby.

"You're lucky he's not measuring my dick because then you'd have to pay for the heart attack it'd give him." Wolf shot a wink at Chance and slapped a smile on his face. He was not going to be a moody bastard anymore today.

XⓄXⓄXⓄXⓄ

Hazel spent a great big giant chunk of time with Claire's mother and sister on FaceTime, showing them every angle of Claire's wedding dress. She looked like a princess. All agreed that white on a redhead was a wonderful combination. There were tears and happy squeals all around. Hazel had to shout a little, because Fancy Pants seemed to be having a music war. The Fancy side had classical music cranked. The Pants side seemed to favor classic rock.

When Claire was finally ready to start pinning for the alterations, she encouraged Hazel to go try on her bridesmaid dress.

After looking at the melon-colored A-line dress, Hazel was grateful her best friend had such impeccable taste. She showed it off to Claire's sister and mother before propping the phone on a chair so she could go get changed.

Hazel latched the dressing room door and started to get undressed. She should have worn or brought a strapless bra for when she tried on the dress. She hadn't thought to ask Claire what kind of neckline she was dealing with.

She toyed with leaving on the black bra but ultimately

decided it would be too distracting for Claire and her family. So Hazel took the bra off, folded it, and set it on top of her shirt on the chair.

She should have worn regular heels, not her fuck-me boots, as well. They were a bitch to lace up. Hazel decided to leave them on while she wrangled herself out of her skirt.

Finally, she was down to her boots and her black thong panties. As she turned at the waist, her heel caught on the throw rug in the dressing room and she started to fall.

Everything moved in slow motion as her brain replayed Lottie's warning about the walls. They looked solid, but they were only temporary dividers papered to look real.

And that's when she ripped right through the wall.

The tearing noise wasn't nearly as loud as she thought it would be, and just before her ass hit the floor, two hands slipped under her arms and grabbed her boobs, halting her fall.

"Oh." Hazel caught her breath. She recognized those hands.

"Holy crap. Are you okay?" Wolf's voice was in her ear over the clash of the loud music. He wasn't nearly as panicked as she was.

She had to rely on him for balance as her heel was still tangled in the throw rug. He put her down on the floor of what had to be his dressing room on the Pants side of Fancy Pants.

"Did you hurt yourself?" Wolf asked as he took a knee to free her foot.

She shook her head. It had all happened so quickly. But she was pretty sure he'd prevented the giant tailbone bruise she might otherwise have had.

She remembered she was topless and covered her boobs. It was far too late, of course, as he had already gotten an eyeful, but she had to give him credit for trying to act like a gentleman. His dressing room was all faux dark leather and steel touches. The Hazel-shaped hole was puckered with what looked like torn heavy paper.

"Oh, they're going to kill me. I just tore through their wall!"

The dressing rooms were enclosed from floor to ceiling, so he was the only one seeing her like this. At least it was a show he'd seen before.

"They better not. That wall isn't even close to safe. Chicks have to get in and out of those complicated dresses in there. They'll deal with me before they get to you." Wolf was adamant.

He held out a hand, and she adjusted her arm to cover both nipples and allowed him to assist her.

He looked away, which gave her a moment to ogle him. Wolf was in just his jeans—no boots and no shirt. It reminded her vaguely of Scott's parting outfit. She wished her vagina would wise up and stop salivating when a male was dressed like that in her presence.

He was also hard. She shouldn't have been looking, but the sex kitten in her had to know if her near-naked state was affecting him.

"My hero," she offered fairly sarcastically.

"Don't be a wise ass." He tried to step back into his own dressing room and tripped over the uneven wall remnants.

Hazel had no choice but to turn her back. He pulled her to him and planted them both on the cushioned bench in his dressing room. She was sitting on his hard-on now.

She watched in the mirror that reflected them as he rolled his eyes and shook his head. "Fate tests me."

She could feel the embarrassment start to curl her shoulders. "I'm sorry. I didn't intend—"

Wolf lifted her and rearranged her as though he did it for a living. He stopped the apology with his mouth. Hazel ended up with her knees on either side of his hips, and his hands everywhere. One was kneading her ass and the other was caressing her right breast.

He was dry humping her, as well. It was as if he'd been waiting days to do just this to her. He stopped kissing her to suck on her other breast.

The mirror behind him and the mirror behind her worked as a visual trampoline. They looked fuckhot like this. She moaned his name.

"Oh God. Please don't make any noise. I can't stand it. My dick is going to die," he pleaded in between sucking and kissing all the skin he could get to. She pinched his nipples hard in return.

Her hair was in his hands now as he kissed from her jaw to her shoulder and went back to bite the base of her neck.

"Look at these goddamned tits." And then his hands were on them. "You in this thong and these boots are an eyegasm. Tell me I can make you come. Please, oh my God."

Having this grumpy, handsome fucker want her made her feel like she had superpowers. She grabbed his hair in response. "If I let you, it better be the best one of my life."

He was kissing her again, his tongue learning exactly what her want tasted like.

Wolf stilled as if he were trying to find his better judgment. They were in public. She'd broken a freaking wall. There was a glass of an amber-colored liquid on the small table in the dressing room. She decided to use it to change his mind.

She sat back on her heels, and he grabbed her ass to keep her steady. She picked up his glass and raised her eyebrow. He watched her every move like a predator about to pounce. She touched the tip of her tongue to the alcohol and licked her lips. Then she put her finger in the glass and dabbed the liquid on her shoulder.

"Clean that up."

He put one hand between her legs and used his knuckle to rub her as he bit the place on her shoulder she'd just touched.

She began moving against his hand. Then she dipped her pinkie in the drink and put a drop on her nipple.

"And this."

He used two hands to move her panties out of the way while he bit and sucked her nipple.

She tossed her head back as the pleasure of his fingers penetrating her combined with the rubbing made her forget she was in a dressing room with a man she was furious with.

He snagged the glass just before she dropped it and set it back on the table. "You like being upside-down?" He pushed on the center of her chest until she was moving backwards, so she was no longer on her knees but lying on his extended legs, which he'd kicked out. His forethought made her shiver.

"Look."

When she did, she could see her topless reflection. And

then he began the work she remembered so well. She watched in the mirror as he pushed her panties to the side and then his three fingers were inside her deep.

"You want the pinkie again?" He was bent over her, chest flexing with his exertions.

She nodded. God help her, she wanted everything he had to give her.

To be nearly naked with this man's carnal scrutiny on her had to be the ingredients for pure greed.

Wolf watched himself in the mirror and looked from her reflection to her on his lap and back again. She couldn't reach him in this position, so she grabbed her breasts instead.

"Yes," he whispered, his nose flaring.

White. She was seeing white. Reflexes had her closing her eyes.

It was too much. She had to be quiet, so she bit her lips together while she writhed. And then he put her over the top. Fingers everywhere with his mouth on her clit, sucking on her. She almost blacked out. Hazel was sure she'd stopped breathing for a minute as she came so hard her chest hurt.

He lifted her up while she still struggled to catch her breath. He hugged her to his chest and kissed her temple. His skin was damp and sweaty, from giving her the sensations that took her to another frigging planet.

Lottie called from the other side, "You okay, Hazel? I'm coming in to help you get dressed!"

"Say no. Say no right now," Wolf demanded.

She was confused for a minute before she put it all together. She was nearly naked. She'd ripped a hole in their wall. Lottie was about to bust in on her whore scene.

"Fine. No. I'm fine. Sorry. I was texting. I'll be out soon." She sounded breathless, but at least she'd said the right words.

Wolf stood and set Hazel on the floor, putting his hand against the door, which thankfully swung in to prevent even Lottie armed with a key from entering.

"Well, hurry up. Your friends are waiting."

Hazel was in an afterglow daze, so Wolf grabbed the dress off the hanger before helping her stand. With an ease that surprised Hazel, he unzipped the bridesmaid's gown, popped it over her head, and zipped it up. He tried to fix her hair but just turned her at the shoulders and pointed at the mirror. She adjusted as best she could.

She looked at his jeans and his fairly prominent man problem. "You're not wet. I know I came?" She was confused. She was a messy comer in general.

He pointed to the door. "Go out there and stall. I'll see what I can do to fix this." He pointed to the ripped wall.

She was still stuck on the fact that he wasn't sticky from her. She pointed to her crotch and then his pants.

He stepped closer and moved her hair out of the way, whispering, "I was ready for you, gorgeous." Then he pulled back and purposely licked all the way around his lips.

He'd swallowed.

Her jaw dropped open. He was amazing.

The slow, sexy grin he gave her in return was everything, even showing a hint of his dimple.

I Think

Wolf watched her leave. That she fell, almost naked, into his dressing room was insane. He wasn't sure what kind of test Hazel was, but he was failing at every turn.

He should have helped her back through the hole she'd created. Instead, he'd been desperate and finger-banged her upside-down.

It was cool. He could be cool. He decided that since she'd taken the blame for his office indiscretion, he would take the blame for this. He got dressed and made sure none of Hazel's clothes were on his side.

Wolf opened the dressing room door and stumbled through, holding his head.

"Holy shit. What the actual fuck? That wall is made of paper? My damn head."

Chance was the first to get to him. "What happened?"

Wolf pointed at the dressing room. "The wall! It's made of paper. You should warn people."

The salesman and tailor on the Pants side were very apologetic, quickly informing the Fancy side that the dressing room was no longer useable. They got Wolf ice for his head, and he pretended that it helped before handing it back on their way to the lobby. The store gave them discounts on the clothes they were ordering and didn't charge for the alcohol they had drunk.

When Hazel appeared, dressed in her black outfit, she'd obviously reapplied her lipstick. Having seen what she was wearing under that black outfit made his blue balls bluer.

Chance patted his back. "If you watch her any harder you're going to give her an X-ray."

Wolf clicked his tongue at his friend.

"So convenient that the dressing room you tore a wall down to get to was hers. But you keep fighting it, brother." Chance left him to kiss Claire.

Peter started chatting up Hazel, letting her know that Wolf had fallen through the wall. Hazel fanned her face and blushed. "So glad I wasn't there. That would have been... interesting."

Peter held the door for Hazel, and Wolf walked through behind her like a possessive asshole.

Claire had ordered a car service, and when the minivan arrived, they all piled in. Hazel spoke to him, and he watched her lips move like a man obsessed.

"I thought that car was yours?" She pointed to the coupe that they had gathered around earlier.

"Nope. We took the Metro to get here. Do as the locals do and all." Wolf wanted to sit next to her and put his arm around her so that Peter would stop looking at his girl.

Shit.

His girl.

He allowed himself to let the future flash in his

imagination. What he could do to Hazel if she were his. In her apartment. Or the apartment he was renting for his stay here in Garville.

He ached in his pants. The swell of her breast was visible, and he wanted to lick it and bite it. Her arm. God, he needed it locked around his neck.

If he didn't get to feel her orgasm around his dick, he really thought he would die. Tasting her was not enough. Not even close.

He glanced at her pretty face; she looked overwhelmed. He realized he was full-out creeper staring at her. Her eyes flicked down to his hand. It was balled in a fist, and he forced himself to relax it. A small smile appeared on her lips with the motion.

Peter was talking to her again, and Wolf spent the time trying to memorize her laugh. And her glances at him. Hazel had him twisted. Obviously, he wanted to fuck her. But seeing Peter try to charm her was bringing out the worst in him.

He hadn't allowed himself to get attached in all these years. Now was not the time to start.

When the car arrived at the restaurant, the place was hopping. There was outdoor dining and rooftop dancing. The Thursday nightlife here was pretty damn impressive.

Of course, Wolf realized how much that sucked when he followed a few strides behind Hazel and saw all the men in the place check her out. No one dared look at Claire with giant, man muscle Chance's hand on her lower back, but Hazel looked single.

Shit.

Hazel *was* single.

When they were all settled in a spot along the wall that had ledge space for drinks, Chance went to the bar to order some. Wolf couldn't let that happen, especially because he wasn't sure there would be time in their busy schedule to allow for a proper bachelor party before the big lug tied the knot.

Wolf managed to catch a server and explain that the entire tab was to be put on his credit card, and he fought with Chance while he explained why the drinks were on him.

When he finally got back to the spot where they'd left Hazel and Claire, he only found Peter. The Booty Camp security man let them know that the girls had gone upstairs to the roof to get some air. After the drinks were handed out, Wolf and Chance took the girls' glasses up to the roof, having their tab transferred up there and ordering some snacks as well.

Claire and Hazel were dancing together. In that sexy way only girls who knew each other very well could do. Obviously, they'd been on many dance floors together.

With a quick glance around, Wolf saw how many men had their eyes locked in on the pair of them. When Wolf stepped behind Hazel and Chance twirled Claire in for a kiss, the stares were averted.

Hazel turned to him. "Oh good! We had to resort to dancing together to make the guys leave us alone."

Wolf bit his lip and pulled her closer under the guise of speaking to her. "Where."

She shivered with his words, which he intentionally breathed on her sensitive neck. She pulled back and looked in his face. "I don't know anymore. I can only see you now."

It was literal, he knew, but it felt much deeper when she looked at him like that.

He nodded instead of saying, *"Same. The fucking same,"* like he should have because Peter was there. He tapped Hazel on the shoulder as a low-key song came on.

"Can I have this dance?" Peter wasn't asking permission from Wolf. Because Hazel wasn't his. "Dancing's cool, right, boss?" Peter smiled. He twirled Hazel away, laughing.

Chance and Claire were already dancing. Peter pulled Hazel close. Wolf saw complete red.

One, of course, Peter was fired. Two, he was going to kill him. Three, it was time to get Peter's hands off Hazel.

Wolf threaded through the crowd of dancers and tapped Peter hard on the shoulder. "Go wait for our snacks."

He stepped between Peter and Hazel. He could finally breathe when she was in his arms again. He shot daggers at Peter. The man had worked for Booty Camp for six months, and tomorrow he would be unemployed. No flirting with the boss's girl.

Hazel put her hand on his cheek. "Hi. Are you planning on showing up to this conversation or no?"

She'd been talking and he'd missed it.

"Sorry, what?" He looked at her now. She was gorgeous. Just devastating. Maybe that was his problem. He spent his time glowering at someone else while ignoring beauty in his arms.

"I was saying it's nice out." She waved her hand in the air.

It was. The restaurant had heaters set up on the roof, and even though it was crowded, it wasn't sweaty. The stars that were visible were striking.

"It is. Great. Did Peter say anything to you?" Wolf looked at their hands grasped together. Her slender fingers looked kissable, but he restrained himself.

"No. Just asked if I was a customer anymore, and I said I wasn't sure." She smiled at Peter, who waved.

"I'm fucking firing him tonight." Wolf glared at his soon-to-be former employee.

She looked concerned and frowned. "He seems super nice. Why the change of heart?"

"Just business." Wolf twirled her to break her seeking eye contact. "Don't concern yourself."

She gave him a half smirk. "Never can tell me everything, right? What if I kissed you right now? How would you react to that?"

He panicked. The last thing he needed was Peter witnessing that.

"I see." Hazel stopped dancing. "I'm great behind closed doors, right?"

"Yes."

She got it. Behind closed doors they could do anything she wanted.

But that was apparently not the answer to help tamp down her mounting anger.

"If you'll excuse me, I have to use the ladies room." She stepped backwards before adding, "Alone."

Wolf watched her storm away. He got it wrong. Again. He went to the table where their drinks were and noticed Peter was gone. And now he was concerned.

Wolf waited for a few minutes while he scanned the

crowd. No Peter. But he did see an unwelcome person. Scott. The ex-boyfriend extraordinaire.

Shit.

Cars And Men

Hazel descended the stairs and tried to figure out what the hell Wolf's deal was. She was damn sick of him being everything she needed between her legs and then a dickhead after.

As she stopped on the landing, Scott was in front of her. "Hey!" he said, apparently exuberant to see her.

She was less so. "Scott."

"You here for the two-for-one mojitos?" He put his arm around her.

"No." She pushed him away.

Behind her, Peter interrupted. "Hey, babe, you ready to go? This guy bothering you?"

Hazel took the out that Peter offered. "Yeah. Thanks. No, Scott lives in my building."

Peter grabbed her hand as though they'd been dating for years. "Let's get out of this place."

Hazel agreed, but she didn't want to actually leave until she'd talked to Claire. It was her friend's night, and she didn't want to pull yet another Cinderella act just because Wolf was being a dick to her once more.

Peter dragged her to the corner of the foyer where diners would wait for a table in the restaurant when there was a dinner service.

"Everything okay?" Peter let go of her hand and smiled at her comfortingly. She wasn't sure why Wolf wanted to fire Peter. He seemed like he would be good at his job.

"Yeah. Thanks, though. I didn't want to have a conversation with that guy." She gestured over her shoulder with her thumb.

Peter put his hand on her shoulder. "I could tell. Gauging a scene is part of what I do best. I pick up on details that a lot of people might miss."

"Lucky me." She felt a vibration next to her breast and pulled her phone out of her bra.

"Wow. Great place to keep that." He didn't give her any creepy leers, so she continued to read the text from Claire.

Where did u go?

She typed in a quick reply of _"bathroom,"_ and refocused on Peter.

"I don't have any pockets tonight, so it will have to do."

"So, did you want a drink or no?" He pulled out his wallet and pointed to the bar.

"I'm good. I think I have a wine upstairs. I really am going to the bathroom now that I'm down here." Hazel started to back up.

"I'll hang out outside. Hard to stop being protective of our clients, if that's what you are." He held out his hand to indicate the direction she should head.

"You know where the bathrooms are?" She was impressed.

"I know where all the visible exits are, too. Second nature." Peter followed behind her as she walked to the left of the bar. She saw Wolf's profile by the stairs. He was obviously searching for someone. She ducked into the ladies room and gave herself a few alone moments to gain her composure and try and make a plan for how she was going to move forward.

She washed her hands and checked her makeup. Dancing had added volume to her hair and pink to her cheeks, so she left her face as it was.

Hazel wasn't leaving on account of Wolf. She was an empowered lady who was allowed to enjoy her orgasms and not have them rule her emotions.

She stepped out of the bathroom to find the very man she'd been steeling herself against there, waiting for her.

Peter was nowhere to be found.

Wolf pushed away from the wall as she came closer. Three guys in the same place giving her the once over should have made her confidence skyrocket, but it just made her nervous.

"Your ex is here," he warned her.

"Yeah. I saw him. But, you know, he only hurt me the one time, so maybe I should go stand with him. I've got better odds with him, statistically speaking, than I do with you." She saw Peter's red hair as he bent to listen to a pretty woman talk in his ear.

He looked concerned and touched her wrist. "He works for me. He can't be interested in you."

"Okay." She folded her arms in front of her. "Maybe I'm just friendly. Can't imagine that, huh? I'm good for more than one thing, Wolfgang."

"You're right. I need to start saying no to all the temptations you offer. But I'm only human." He looked around the restaurant again.

"Oh, because I'm such a tempting whore, right?" Hazel crossed her arms in front of her.

He stopped looking around and pressed her against the wall with his nearness. He ran his hand from the top of her hair to her cheek before stroking his thumb along her jawline.

"It's because my heart stops when you want me. And I have to touch you to breathe again." Wolf grazed her bottom lip tenderly.

He wrecked her determination, his words making her brain stumble.

She leveled him with a stare she hoped she'd be proud of later. "Then you better shape up, Wolf."

He stepped backwards and made room for her as she left to go back upstairs.

Wolf... he was the one who would hurt the worst. Far worse than Scott. Because he felt so right that walking away from him was actually painful.

XOXOXOXO

Wolf watched her walk away with her head held high. And because he couldn't stop himself, he watched as Peter's head swiveled around to locate Hazel.

179

Wolf stepped forward to follow her when Scott, the classless ex, was in front of him. He had to watch Peter leave the honey he was talking to and trot up the stairs behind Hazel.

He adjusted his gaze to take in Scott. "So, it looks like you lucked out. Broke up already?"

The man wasn't drunk. His eyes were clear.

"We're not together. But that doesn't open any doors for you."

"Cool. Because I think you need to step away from her if that's the case." Scott put his chin in the air, fight in his eyes.

"She's a client. We take care of our own." Wolf moved to step around him.

"And then you roll out when? How long does your sex circus stay in town again?" Scott widened his eyes.

"*Sex circus?*" Wolf made a fist. "You know what? I think you've mistaken me for someone who gives a fuck."

Before Wolf could take his rage out on Scott's face, Chance was between them. "Hey. Hey. Hey! Let's knock this off for a minute." Chance's size brings both men down a peg or two without even trying. "Can I get you a drink, son? Let's go to the bar." Chance manhandled Scott in a way that gave the man no other choice, the whole time talking to him like they were best buds.

Wolf knew Chance was managing Wolf and his anger. Which was part of the reason he got paid such a large salary. Chance had incredible people skills. Wolf was less inclined in that direction.

He ignored Chance and Scott as he watched them toast mojitos.

Wolf walked through the room and acknowledged a few friendly greetings from the single girls in the crowd. He took the stairs two at a time, ready to fight off Peter one more time when he saw Hazel and Claire slow dancing.

He stepped to the side of the crowd and felt Peter sidle up next to him. "That's a pretty sight. Is it illegal to put that mental picture in the spank bank?" Peter smiled.

Wolf didn't say anything else, but inside he was busy not raging at Peter. He needed to stop acting like a rabid version of his nickname. He needed to find some chill.

Chance was at his elbow faster than he expected. "Your friend went home."

"Awesome. That's what we use your superpowers for." Wolf accepted the beer bottle that Chance offered both him and Peter. They toasted to the upcoming wedding, and all three kept their eyes on the girls, who were obviously having a heart-to-heart while swaying to the music.

"I had to offer him a spot on this week's dating panel for a reduced price," Chance said when Peter left to play darts on the other side of the rooftop dance floor.

"And now you're fired." Wolf smiled wryly into the distance.

"Well, if good 'ol Scott finds his match, maybe he won't come sniffing around anymore and you won't have to deal with the competition. Not that you're interested in her, of course." Chance tapped his glass beer bottle to Wolf's.

"You sneaky-assed Booty Camp ninja." Wolf took a sip to complete the toast.

"I've got skills, brother. Time to realize what you got here." Chance started dancing as the music picked up.

Wolf refused to acknowledge him, so Chance made his way over to the ladies and started dancing with them both.

Wolf found a high stool by a bar table and started peeling the label off his beer. It was an old habit. He finished his beer and tried to avoid checking Hazel out. The waitress brought another round, and Wolf drank it pretty quickly.

It'd been a while since he'd been in a crowd like this—one that hadn't paid for the privilege of having him analyze them. There were actually very few good matches in the crowd. There was a reason he was successful at Booty Camp. People had to be open to receive someone else in their life. Chance and Claire had a glorious match. Harmony was the biggest energy they put off.

He looked at Hazel as she held her mojito above her head and shook her ass. She was more open than when he'd met her a few weeks ago. Her energy was less battered. After finding out what she did for a living, he understood the gold energy she had. It took something special to see the potential in all people. To fight for them when they needed a boost. She had that.

Scott had broken her, but she'd healed more than she probably realized when she walked into Booty Camp for the first time. But maybe Wolf was confused. Maybe what he took as needing a match was really her openness to all kinds of people.

He stood up and navigated the dance floor. There was a girl that was in sync, energy wise, with another girl on the side of the dance floor. Both were on the shorter side, so he was willing to bet that one didn't know the other was even there.

What he was about to do was what his mother and grandmother lived for. For two energies like these to not connect because of the physical barriers between them would be a goddamned shame.

He approached the one lady, who watched him with a wary face. Obviously, men weren't her type, but that probably didn't stop them from trying to get with her on a night like this. She was very pretty.

He leaned down and whispered, "If I could tell you that the person who could make your future complete was here tonight, how would you feel about that?"

She looked over the dance floor. "I doubt she's here." The woman met his eyes, letting the information that she was gay sink in.

"She's here. And I don't know if she knows she's looking for you, either. If you feel me." Wolf held out his hand.

Recognition swept across her wary face. "You mean she needs to meet the right person?"

"And you're that person. If we move quickly enough." Wolf looked at his own hand. "What's your name?"

"Brenda." She took his hand. "I can't believe I'm doing this. Know that I can kick your ass if this is some shitty trick."

"It's not. You're a better judge of people than you give yourself credit for." Wolf led the way, finding the small blonde in the corner with her friends.

Wolf interrupted the conversation. He got a little tongue-tied. This was why he preferred matchmaking in the more scientific method. It felt so... personal when he made a match like this. He'd done it so few times.

"Can I talk to you?" Wolf held his hand out to her. She gave him a look that clearly said *fuck you* until she saw Brenda.

He watched as the breath left her lungs. She took his hand, and he felt a bolt of electricity go through him. From one woman to the other. No one would ever see it or know it. But it recharged Wolf all over again.

He felt his ancestors then. The bubble around the three of them was almost mystical. Thrilling, for sure.

Wolf led them through the crowd and below so they could get to know each other where the music wasn't so loud.

He peeked over his shoulder at them and they were both blushing.

By the time he got them downstairs and ordered them each a glass of champagne, Wolf could have fallen off the planet and they would never have noticed.

He was standing between them the moment they fell in love. He would always be a part of their origin story.

Wolf backed away and watched from a distance for a minute.

They were glowing, the two of them. Brenda and the blonde—her name was Samantha—had gone from a singular to a plural because he'd recognized that they belonged together.

He turned to go back upstairs, wanting Hazel in his arms. Fuck his own rules. She made him feel like he wanted to be a plural, too.

When he got to the top of the stairs, he couldn't find her. He saw Peter.. Claire and Chance were snuggling, but Hazel was gone.

BR♥KEN

Hazel sat in the back of the cab. No tears anymore. No feeling anymore. To see Wolf take not one, but two women downstairs told her all she needed to know about him.

He was great in bed, of that she was sure. But that wasn't enough to keep stabbing herself in the heart with disappointment for.

Enough was enough. For real this time. He was a player and a user. He talked a great game. But she was betting that was his thing. Like a traveling salesman with a girl in every port, he could charm and infuriate her all day until his shit show moved to the next city.

It was time to let time do its work on her. Fix what she had broken by trusting two douchebag men.

She paid the cab driver when she got to her apartment building. The rain started as she dashed to the front door.

After Hazel was in her building and out of her elevator, she fielded another text from Claire, who'd understood when she saw how devastated Hazel had been by Wolf leading two women downstairs like Mick Jagger in his heyday.

She even helped Hazel find the side stairs off the rooftop

that were obviously only for emergencies.

And getting away had been an emergency.

Hazel locked her door and went into her apartment. She wasn't leaving it until work on Monday. She had her money back. Scott was out of her life, and now Wolf was, too.

Hazel went to her fridge and grabbed the wine she didn't need. She had to get out of her boots. Her feet wanted to die and kiss her after they were free. Those were not dancing boots.

Hazel drew herself a nice hot bath with bubbles and picked her favorite playlist from her phone. She set her wineglass on the edge of the tub, dropped her outfit on the floor, and slipped into the bath.

She refused to cry about that man one more time.

Hazel rested low in the bubbles before dunking her head under the water. She would have to toss in the leave-in conditioner after she was done.

That mundane thought comforted her. Because hair needed to be conditioned.

Men didn't need their dicks sucked. And maybe her upside-down orgasms with Wolf were important, but her hair wouldn't suffer if she forgot to do that act.

She got through four songs before the water turned tepid, so she ran the shower to rinse off and apply her conditioner.

His touch was gone now. Again.

She put on her softest sleep shorts and her sleep tank and worked a brush through her long hair. It was a soothing habit. After that, there was moisturizer.

So many things to keep her busy. Hazel checked her messages and saw that Claire had sent a few, which she responded to. She distracted Claire with ideas about the upcoming wedding and a promise to spend some serious Pinterest time together.

Another text popped up from a number she didn't recognize.

You ran. I thought we had a moment.

She knew it was Wolf, but two could play at being a dickhead.

Sorry. Is this Scott, Peter, or Grant?

Hazel didn't know a Grant, but that was fine.

Now you're just making me jealous for no damn reason.

Don't know who this is, so I'm blocking this number.

No. Don't. It's me. Wolf.

Now I'm really blocking this number.

How could you leave without telling me?

She was three clicks away from blocking him. But her rage flared up despite all her everyday tasks designed to calm her down.

It was hard to get in there between and your two

bitches.

Then she blocked him.
Fuck him.
Well, no. No fucking him.
He was a dick face. Dickey McDickface, and her father did not raise a daughter to be a booty call for a douche banana with a dumb business named Booty Camp.

Hazel looked at the ceiling as her traitorous memory brought up the counterargument of his kisses. And his fingers. And his mouth. And the moment outside the bathroom where he legit seemed devastated by the presence of her.

A new number beeped through.

They weren't my bitches.

Oh for fuck's sake. Whose phone did you steal? Blocking this number.

She did just that.
Claire popped through again with a picture of a picture from the internet showing a pretty melon-colored table display.

Hazel typed an idea.

Hey if you can get a big screen, you should do a slideshow of pictures of you guys.

Claire was super excited about the idea and they traded

favorite songs until another number popped up.

I was making a match. You inspired me.

She took a picture of her middle finger and sent it to the number before she blocked it.

Claire sent a picture of some bouquets. Very pretty white roses.

Another unknown number popped up.

I'm running out of humans I can demand a phone from. The girls were together. As a match. They were meant for each other. The ladies you saw me with.

Hazel swallowed. She interacted with Claire a few more times but didn't block the last number right away.

Again it forced itself on her screen.

I meant what I said to you. You're exceptional. You're the reason I made a match just for the sake of making one. Instead of for profit.

She ignored the message and went back to texting Claire, commenting on the bouquet suggestions she had.

Seeing Claire in her dress tonight really made it hit home that her best friend was getting married. She'd always expected to double date with Claire and a boyfriend for a few more years. Never a whirlwind situation for her practical, but crazy friend.

I want to see you.

She tossed her wet hair around and pulled it into a loose bun on top of her head.

Did you block this number?

She let her phone sit on her lap and took another sip of her wine. He was asking to be invited back into her hopes.

Shit. Now I have to steal a phone.

She picked up the phone and typed.

Not blocked.

That's good. Can you feel me smiling? That's really good.

She pictured the dimple hinting on the side of his white smile.

Don't throw yourself a parade yet.

Can I come by your place?

You're too forward.

You know what? I understand that. That's fine. I'll trade phones with this girl forever because I want to remain unblocked.

Hazel laughed and bit her lips shut. He was worming his way back in. She sucked at setting boundaries.

Though I would really appreciate it if you would unblock the first number because I don't have my mom's number memorized and I could get in a lot of trouble if I never speak to her again. She's already pretty pissed at me anyway, though.

Hazel unlocked her phone and unblocked the first number.
She texted him the word:

Fine.

Then she named him Humping Wolf Pup in her contacts and sent him a screen shot so he could see what she'd done on her phone.

I can see you missed me, too.

She considered the text for a minute. The whole thing reminded her of when they were writing on the tablecloth.

Trusting you is the issue. I never know which Wolf I'm getting.

I'm sorry about that. Really.

She didn't respond.

Blocked?

No. Not yet.

Good. Can I come over?

She thought about that for a few minutes. She knew what would happen. She and Wolf would wind up in her bed. She had to respect that pain he'd put her through for a little longer.

No. Not yet.

Okay.

She could feel his sadness. But she wanted him to be serious about coming to see her. Not falling into a dressing room half naked. Not making impulse decisions in his office.

Good night.

Sweet dreams, Hazel.

XOXOXOXO

The next day, Claire came over to make the war board for the wedding. Teachers planning a wedding had to be the scariest thing on the planet. Their inherent love of schedule and details turned Hazel's living room into a scene from "Ocean's Eleven."

They both had their laptops, phones, and iPads pulled up to various wedding sites.

"We basically have to do two years' worth of work in about a week." Claire took a gulp of her coffee. She'd brought Hazel a cup, as well.

Putting Wolf as far out of her mind as she could was the perfect prescription for today. He'd sent a few texts and she'd responded, but they didn't get a full-blown conversation going.

She knew where he was, anyway. Chance and Wolf had to take a day trip to the next city on the tour to scope out the rental space that was lined up. Booty Camp was like a rock band on tour with all the details they had to iron out.

By the time Claire and Hazel were hungry for lunch, they'd nailed down the invites, the flowers, and the table settings. The afternoon held arranging an officiant, a DJ, and a photographer. They needed sustenance to make that happen.

When they got to the lobby to take their break at the local deli, Scott was there.

He was dressed in all black and was wearing his shades on his head. He looked good and he knew it.

Scott almost stumbled when he saw Hazel. "Oh. Hey. Hazel. So great to see you. How are you?"

Hazel tilted her head one way then the other. "Fine. Thanks for asking."

"You know your friend set me up with a discount for Booty

Camp! Maybe we can go on a date!" He shuffled into the waiting elevator, and Hazel felt her pupils turn into lasers.

"Really? Really? Wolf invited Scott to Booty Camp?" She ground her teeth together.

Claire frowned. "I don't know what's up with him. That's crazy. I know he knows who Scott is."

Hazel stomped and fumed out the door. "I swear the second I give that man a chance, he pisses on it."

She pulled out her phone and texted one word to Wolf.

BLOCKED!

And then she went ahead and did that very thing.

He was hanging on by a thin thread with her, and this tipped him over.

Claire put her arm around Hazel. "Don't be too mad. He's trying. I really think he is."

Hazel widened her eyes at her friend. "Are you taking his side?"

Claire scoffed, "Of course not. For God's sake. I'm always on your side. I just happen to know Chance considers Wolf a brother for good reasons."

"Bromances are strange things. It doesn't mean Wolf isn't a player." Hazel pulled open the door to the deli.

Claire got on the end of the line. "How much has Wolf told you about his mom and grandmother?"

"Not much." Hazel's answer was clipped.

"Well, what he's doing with the matchmaking—they disapprove. He really wants to make them proud, but they don't agree with him doing the Camp at all." Claire flicked

Hazel's hair off her shoulder and straightened her jacket collar.

"So, I should let him take a giant shit all over my heart repeatedly?" Hazel stomped a foot.

Claire covered her mouth. "Language, lady. We're in public."

Hazel licked the palm of Claire's hand, which she pulled away.

"Of course not. Like I said, I'm always on your side. It's just..." Claire's argument died before she made it.

"What?" Hazel stepped forward in line.

"I think you guys kind of sparkle together. Your," she whispered, "sexual tension gives people around you sympathy blue balls."

Hazel wrestled Claire a little and covered her mouth now. "Language."

Claire laughed as she pulled away. "I would just hate for you to rush out of something that might be good because you're afraid Scott wasn't a fluke or a one-time heartbreak. That you think history keeps repeating itself."

Hazel bought some time by fixing her hair. The bad thing about having a best friend who knew you so long was that she could cut to the bone.

"I'm not trying to hurt you. You know that. I just want you to give this a fair shot." Claire stepped up to order, but before she did she added, "There's a time limit on this one."

Hazel exhaled and tried to focus on the menu on the wall while she pictured Wolf's lips in her imagination.

Claire gave Hazel some peace while they spent the rest of the evening making more plans. They got a lot accomplished.

Claire had to leave after an order-in salad dinner. Hazel promised to meet Chance and Claire at the theater tomorrow for a cake tasting. The baker was meeting them with several selections. Claire mentioned that Wolf was staying on in the next Booty Camp tour city for an extra evening.

ThE TasTiNG

Hazel had agreed to join Claire and Chance to offer them another opinion on the cake tasting, so she put on her favorite jeans, which had just a few tears, and paired them with nude heels, a white sweater, and vintage leather jacket. Red lips and soft hair made her feel like she could face the world despite the fact that she could easily spend a few days in leggings and a tank top eating ice cream and flipping the middle finger at any man who appeared on the TV.

When she arrived at the theater, she texted Claire to let her in. Chance was the one to actually open the door and he offered a hug.

Claire was in Chance's version of a rented office, which was across the lobby from Wolf's closed office door. Hazel did her best not to look too hard at the door.

Chance pulled an extra chair up to his desk, and Claire and he watched as she tasted the four flavors the baker had left on Chance's desk just before he'd left.

Claire had her iPad displayed with her wedding planning pictures on it. Hazel loved the moist vanilla cake with the buttercream frosting, and Chance and Claire seemed pleased that had been her choice.

Chance kissed Claire, grabbed a folder, and went out into the lobby. When the door swung open, Hazel saw that the Booty Camp staff had assembled while she'd been talking taste and flavor combinations with the bride- and groom-to-be.

"Is it a date night?" Hazel pointed at the now closed door.

"Yeah. They're having a clean up night, where they bring in some new people to try and match up the stragglers who are still unmatched from previous events." Claire flipped through a book of cake designs, making notes on the pad next to it.

Hazel wanted to ask where the hell Wolf was if it was a date night, and Claire looked up from her cake studies to pin her with a look.

"He did the matches and sent the names to Chance."

"Oh." Hazel looked at her hands.

"Not that you're wondering, right?" Claire wiggled her eyebrows.

"I'm not. I was. But I'm trying to not." Hazel stood. "Are you good? I should probably get out of here. People might recognize me from my various outbursts and nudity." Hazel picked up her jacket from where she'd left it on the back of her chair.

Claire distracted her with a few more cake pictures, but it was clear that her friend was a fan of the classic design with live flowers, so once Hazel pointed that out, she was allowed to leave.

The girls hugged, and Hazel slipped on her leather jacket. When she got to the lobby, she was plunged into darkness.

After a few staggering, disoriented steps, she heard a friendly female voice in her ear. "Okay, here's your blindfold. Hang tight."

Hazel vaguely made out the woman's Booty Camp staff T-shirt in a flash of light from the other side of the lobby.

Chance's voice came over the loudspeaker. "Please, remain still. The darkness helps us stay in touch with the senses that really matter when seeking a person to spend time with. You'll have to get to know the person without any of society's pesky preconceived notions getting in the way of the match."

Hazel tried to fight off the Booty Camp staff member politely, but it was pointless. The chick could seriously look into Dominatrix work on the side. The blindfold was secured tightly in mere seconds.

"Stay here and we'll match you in one moment."

"Hi, I'm not here for a match, I want to just go out the front door."

There was no response. Hazel tried to undo the knot or slide the fabric off her head, but it was stuck tight.

As she tried to work on the knot, Hazel realized the Dominatrix-in-training had included quite a bit of her hair in her sailor's knot. Hazel amended the woman's profession from sex worker to a dock cruise ship securing specialist. The knot was some sort of wonder.

There were no clear strips to start with.

She was passed around by encouraging Booty Camp workers who seemed confused who her match was. Her protests about not actually being a client and wanting to get out the door were hushed and handled as if they were first time jitters. She tried standing still, but the forced blindness was overwhelming. She overheard someone say there was an extra customer and that they should start by matching her up with him.

Then the Booty Camp staff member who gave her the last direction told her it was a dark date and reminded them to whisper to each other. Hazel stopped trying to explain that her hair was tied in this dumb knot and gave up. She knew the Booty Camp drill. She just needed to make small talk—well, small whispers—with a guy, and then she could get someone to help with her hair. Maybe even her mystery date could help her.

She was guided into a plush chair and someone sat down next to her.

They got the go ahead to begin whispering.

Hazel didn't even let him introduce himself, though she did whisper. She was sick of being the Booty Camp spectacle.

"Hi. I'm not supposed to be here. My hair is caught in this knot, and the lady wouldn't listen to me when I told her I was just walking through the lobby to leave." She could feel the guy next to her because there wasn't even an inch of personal space between them.

He chuckled and whispered back, "Figures. That's my luck. I come to the famous Booty Camp and get set up with a girl who's just trying to get the heck out of here."

She laughed a little. "I'm sorry. That's usually my kind of luck, too. You'll meet someone great here."

"Are you a alumni or something?" He had a nice whisper.

"You could say that. I've seen a lot of people make matches here. That's not how it worked for me, though." She tried working at the knot and accidentally elbowed the man next to her before putting her hands back in her lap. "Sorry!"

"It's okay. You want me to try and help with the knot? I used to be a Boy Scout." He touched her hand with a fumbling gesture. "Here, put my hand where the knot is."

Hazel thought about it for a minute but decided to take his help. She guided his hand to the back of her head.

"Wow. You have long hair. And it's all twisted up in here. Can you turn a little so I can reach it with both hands?" he whispered.

"Sure." She twisted at the waist.

"My blindfold is way too tight, as well. Before they paired us up, I tried to get mine off. I think that lady who did mine was a Boy Scout, too." He laughed at his own joke.

Hazel laughed as well. She swore the place was cursed and told him as much. He didn't seem to be making any progress with the knot.

A few things happened at the same moment. She heard Wolf's voice, she decided that she could probably help her date out of his blindfold so he could help her better and she turned to face him, and his hands dropped from the back of her head to her chest as she turned.

Her mystery man full-on honked her boobs.

N♡T Ha3El Again

For Wolf, the night was not a success. He'd left the next tour spot, Marren Hotel, unhappy. He had a few clients with mobility issues on this next stop, and their wheelchair accommodations were for shit. They claimed that they met the requirements of the law. But they were not up to Wolf's standards.

Safta Warren, the owner of the venue, clearly didn't think Wolf knew what the hell he was talking about when he told her the doorways were far below the code and almost all of their stairs had no accessibility at all. Wolf had stayed an extra night to hear Safta's last-ditch efforts to keep Booty Camp as a client. The ramps she wanted to rent were cheap shit. He remembered wheeling his sister on one of those temporary tin accessibility jokes. There was no support, and the bounce had made his sister nervous.

So he cancelled his contract with Safta and the Warren building. Chance might actually strangle him for a few minutes. Wolf would have to find a new venue site on his own because Chance was trying to get married, so this kink in his well-oiled machine would be something Wolf needed to work on by himself.

When he arrived, it was dark and the whisper dates were in progress. Chance gave him a quick handshake.

"Back early, brother?" Chance handed Wolf the clipboard he'd been working off of with a small flashlight, rating the compatibility of the dates in progress. "Don't trust me or are you here to check up on Hazel's ex?"

Wolf looked from the clipboard to the dates. "Well, I trust you, so make of that what you will."

Wolf found Scott's blindfolded head on a couch with his flashlight beam. He was next to a girl and seemed to be working on the back of her blindfold. Which was technically not allowed on this date. Wolf passed the clipboard back to Chance. "That bastard's already doing crap wrong."

Wolf started in the direction of Scott and got the sinking, ball-tapping feeling he always got when he saw her.

The girl in the blindfold seated next to Scott was Hazel.

She'd come to Booty Camp to go on another date. She'd blocked his number and then come to find another man while he was gone.

Wolf was instantly angry at Chance for letting it happen. Then he was dangerously jealous.

Hazel turned to face Scott, and the man's hands went from the back of her head to grab a firm hold of Hazel's gorgeous goddamned tits.

"Motherfucker." Wolf half jumped over a few sets of legs, watching the action on the couch that seemed to get further away with every step.

And Wolf heard Scott say, with his goddamned blindfold on, "Wait, is that you Hazel? I'd recognize these jugs anywhere!"

Hazel's mouth dropped open, and she pulled away. Scott held onto her breasts like they were a life raft and he was drowning.

Wolf finally got to the couch at the same time as his eyes adjust to the dim room, knocked Scott's hands off Hazel, and tossed him off the couch onto his ass.

Hazel grabbed her own breasts in defense and confusion. Wolf immediately had flashbacks to his office when she'd done the same thing while lying naked on his desk.

Chance was instantly between Wolf and his prey, Scott. The groom-to-be put a hand on Wolf's chest. "You attend to her. I've got him."

Wolf stepped against the pressure Chance was putting on him like there was no obstacle. He was going to beat the life out of Scott.

Peter swung past Wolf and spoke to Hazel as she tried to get the blindfold off.

That was the only thing that kept Scott's teeth in his head—the fact that Wolf wasn't sharing Hazel and Peter would be too happy to help her out right now.

Wolf turned and tapped Peter out, giving him the hand signal for "get the hell out of here."

Wolf bent low and spoke to her. "Hey, Hazel. It's Wolf. Your hair is caught in this blindfold."

She took a swing at his face, and he was able to back up at the last second so her punch missed his jaw.

"Did you plan this?" She tried to hit him again, but he grabbed her wrists.

"No. No! Are you kidding?" He held Hazel and looked

around the room until he pinned Alison with a stare. "I need scissors." Alison waved her hands and ran off to his office.

"Oh no you don't. You get me Claire. She's in Chance's office. You're not coming near me with sharp things." Hazel kicked out her foot and tried to connect with his shin.

This chick was pissed and feisty. And it gave him the start of some embarrassing wood.

Alison returned with the scissors. He grabbed them and slid them in his back pocket. He looked around the room. The fun whisper event had changed. He picked Hazel up, and she was livid.

"Don't you dare manhandle me, Wolf! I will kick you in balls so damn much."

He hoisted her up and held her close. "You're wrecking the vibe. Just come with me." He didn't really give her a choice.

After he walked through his office door, he kicked it shut and put her on her feet.

She started punching his chest.

"If you don't stand still, you're going to lose a large chunk of your hair." He waited until she stood still. She was frowning but at least stopped being a moving target. He carefully placed the scissors near her temple after smoothing her hair out of the way. He snipped the blindfold off; it had been way too tight. He needed to have a discussion with his staff. They didn't need a damn lawsuit for cutting off the circulation to someone's head.

When Hazel was able to see him and the scissors were away from her head, she started punching him again.

"Was this your plan? Is this how you handle having your number blocked?" She backed up and put her hands in her hair. "My hair is screwed, and you let me get felt up by my ex? What kind of evil bastard are you?"

Wolf liked her mad. Which wasn't even cool, he knew. But the way her face was flushed and her eyes flashed at him was alluring. He had to make her understand that he would never put a woman in that position, least of all her, but instead he watched her struggle with the knot in her hair.

She finally stopped trying and let her hands fall to her sides. The anger shifted into hurt and disappointment as her eyes filled with moisture.

Wolf put the scissors back on his desk. "Did you come here to be put on a date?"

She rolled her eyes and flared her nostrils. "No! By everything that is holy, I got my money back, I'm done. I was here to help Claire and Chance pick out a cake flavor. I didn't even know it was date night. When I tried to leave, I got wrapped in a blindfold and Scott honked my boobs. I really feel like this might be a waking nightmare."

"Do you want me to go out there and beat him up?" Wolf offered the only thing his jealously could think of.

"No. Dickhead. I want you to beat *you* up." She crossed her arms in front of her chest. "And Claire said you wouldn't even be here."

"Is that what you want? To not run into me?" Wolf leaned against the desk, not advancing on her and kissing her until her anger turned to lust.

"I don't know what to make of you. Or any of this deception." She gave a sigh that kind of said it all. She was frustrated.

"I'm not trying to deceive you." He waited until her eyes

were on his. The connection between them was hot. It was undeniable. Maybe even predestined.

"My head tells me you're up to no good. And I'm terrified that I doubt that. What are you even?" Her clear blue eyes searched his.

Her change from feisty and struggling to serious made him feel even guiltier for enjoying her anger.

"I'm into you." He shrugged. That seemed like the safest way to tell her she was literally on his mind every damn second. And that the second he saw Scott touch her, he became a murdering caveman. She had no idea that with the flick of her pretty little finger, he would go out there and decimate the guy, which would lead to his first trip to jail and the demise of his business.

But if she teared up over Scott, it was going down.

"I wouldn't trick you into hanging with him. Ever." Wolf pushed away from the edge of the desk and took a few steps toward her.

She took a step backward. "Well, I didn't come here to go on a date. And I was a little disappointed I wouldn't see you. Why are you back so soon?"

She still had her arms crossed in front of her chest, so he was still close to tipping off the edge of sanity for her. If Scott had hurt her...

"Are you okay"—he gestured to her chest—"there?"

She looked down. "Yeah. I'm fine. Just embarrassed."

That was good enough for Wolf. It was time to kill Scott. He turned to head out of the office, and the only thing that could stop him was her hand on his bicep.

"Don't. It wasn't on purpose."

He looked back at her. She was devastating tonight. The makeup, the outfit. It was all amazing. Well, except for the giant knot and blindfold caught in her long hair.

"I'm not sure I care about his intentions. It was the fact that it happened." He looked down at her hand, and she removed it.

He could almost see the decision to change the topic in order to divert his anger happen in her head.

"Why did you come back tonight? Were you tasting the cake, too?"

His dirty mind went wild. And by cake she meant, well, her lady cake—in his imagination, anyway.

"No. The venue wasn't handicapped accessible. That doesn't work for us. They don't get my money if they don't have a way for people with mobility issues to participate. Now, I have about two weeks to find a new spot to bring the tour and update all the applicants and vendors." Wolf wanted to hug her. And kiss the top of her head. And take her to the lobby and dry hump her while Scott was made to watch with his eyes taped open.

None of those things were happening now, but he got to watch the surprise register in her eyes. "Wow. That's... cool of you."

He ran a hand down his face instead of touching hers the way he wanted to. "My sister couldn't have visited that place if she were still with us. So they have to deal with their own choices. Booty Camp puts places on the map. I'm not giving them publicity if they don't have a good setup for everyone."

She lapsed back into the professional she was. "I always have to investigate that before I take my kids on class trips anywhere. They get super disappointed when they don't get to the stuff the other kids get to do because there is no way for them to get into a building."

Wolf nodded. This was obviously common sense that not everyone possessed.

The silence between them became loud as they seemed to realize at the same time that a core belief they shared matched up. Common ground beyond the obvious physical attraction.

"You're different than I thought you were. Maybe. I have concerns." Her defenses had fallen just a little. The soft part of her that he could see now was even more compelling than her anger.

He risked another step in her direction.

She put up her hand to ward him off. "I think I need a breather. From you. From this." Hazel touched her lips before continuing. "I can't have a fling with you. Because of the way you give me butterflies and kiss me better than I've ever been kissed."

Wolf watched as she took the risk of telling him that she was afraid she liked it all too much. He had the same fear.

She continued, "And you need to respect these things. Please don't use me as a layover during Booty Camp."

Wolf took a step back. And he knew she would think he was admitting her fears were true, not that he had those same ones.

He was cursed to not find a match. Hazel was just another cruel reminder that he'd exploited the family talent to make money. He believed in karma, and walking to the office door and accepting that she was leaving was his way of allowing karma to have her way with him.

Hazel, her hair a wreck in the back as she left his office, cuddled herself as if he'd hurt her worse than Scott had.

The minute he closed the door behind her, he knew he'd made a horrible mistake.

Him Again

Hazel left, satisfied she was in a good place in her head. She'd stood up for her heart and the way Wolf made her feel. She didn't want to take a chance to get hurt again. She couldn't be a booty call for the Booty Camp owner. It would be too personal. It would be the kind of thing that would shape how she felt about men—hell, it had already done that.

Hazel neatened up the living room while repeating her arguments out loud to the empty room. She was heading to her bedroom to change into her pajamas when her intercom buzzed.

She knew it would be Wolf. Before she even heard his voice. She hit the button. "Yeah?"

"It's me."

Deep voice. She pictured him breathing the words into the speaker below.

She hit the unlock button and unlocked her front door, waiting for him by it.

It would lead to sex. There was no doubt about it. She couldn't trust herself in an apartment alone with him.

She argued with herself while she waited. She was young

and allowed to experiment. He was hot as the goddamned sun and the worst crush she'd ever had. And lastly, he'd broken her hope so much in the short time they'd known each other, she felt like she had practice. All her realizations of just a few minutes ago crashed and burned. He'd come for her.

A soft knock put her into motion. She peeked through the peephole. But it was Scott, not Wolf.

She questioned her sanity. Scott would never ring the intercom. Hazel opened the door.

"Scott. What are you doing here?"

The elevator sounded as the doors open. Wolf stepped into the hallway. Black jacket, dark jeans, a goddamned scarf, and a ball cap pulled low.

He lifted his chin and looked at Scott.

Hazel expected Wolf to get angry. Or accuse her of baiting him somehow.

Instead he walked right up to her, put his hands on her face, and kissed her deeply.

Scott made a shocked noise.

Wolf reached out a hand and grabbed Scott's flannel shirt. He stopped kissing Hazel just long enough to say, "Leave," to Scott before stepping on either side of Hazel's body to walk her back into the apartment.

He slammed the door behind them and began kissing her again. His mouth tasted like beer in a manly way.

She pushed back a little. "Hello to you, too."

Wolf pointed at the door. "Does he have a key?"

She shook her head.

Wolf was on her again, pushing her until she was lying

back on the couch.

Hazel had to wait to address him until he was nuzzling her breasts through her white sweater.

"So you just come in here?"

That question made him look up. The look in his eyes was ravenous.

"You would never have let me in if you didn't want me inside your body." He ran his hand down her side, gripping her thigh when he got there.

"Oh, fuck it." Hazel hooked her legs around his waist and pulled him against her. "Kiss me more."

His eyes narrowed. He took her request seriously. "Sit up." He made sure he wasn't pinning her down so she could do as she was told.

Wolf straddled her, and he kissed her, just kissed her, not letting her use her hands on him. Her jaw, her cheek, her ear, the hollow of her neck. He took forever nipping, never wet, just enough.

She'd never been kissed in a way that was this sexy before. The cologne he had on, just a hint that was wrapped in the fabric of his black shirt—she could feel it becoming iconic in her memory right at that moment.

Her mouth, he kissed her mouth, and by then he could have had anything he wanted from her body, but he only wanted her lips. He freed one of her hands so he could wrap his fist around her hair and use it to gently guide her head.

Her free hand was not shy.

First the jacket. She forced him to take off the one sleeve that wasn't on his busy hand. He stopped holding her wrist captive enough to let the material slide down and off. But he wouldn't let go of her hair.

The only thing that made him hesitate was when she searched for his dick. He inhaled and his eyes widened before he went back to her mouth.

When he was kissing her neck again, she whispered, "I think I owe you. For the dressing room.

He stopped and sat back. "Never say you owe me. You are a fucking gift. Every time you let me touch you. Remember that."

Fierce. He seemed determined for her to know he thought highly of her. He wanted to use both of his hands on her, so she was able to feel him. His hard chest, his strong biceps.

She kissed him back, taking a cue from his playbook. Hazel focused all her time on his lips and face. His neck was delicious. He had a bit of five o'clock shadow, so she ran the tip of her tongue over that.

She was breathless with his attention; he'd added her breasts to his choreography.

She began moaning when he touched her hypersensitive nipples.

Hazel had screwed a few boyfriends before. This was nothing like that. He shrugged off his jacket.

She was able to push his shirt aside so she could feel his skin and indents of muscle. She ran her fingers over his nipples, slid her hands behind his back, and leaning forward so she could see the muscles there move as he worked at bringing her an experience.

Wolf stopped. "Can I take you to the bedroom?"

She made a noise that wasn't a word, but an affirmation.

Her grabbed her hair into a ponytail and stood,

encouraging her gently to walk next to him with his other arm around her waist.

It was the slowest pace ever because Wolf was taking time to kiss her more, to feel the parts of her that sitting on the couch had protected.

In the haze of her almost frenzied need for him, she realized it was a skill. This thing he was doing to her, exciting all the parts of her body. He treated her lower back as if it was the most sensual place on her body until, of course, his mouth brought her attention back to the sensitive part of her neck.

After all the time in the world—in which he never touched her between her legs—he told her to crawl onto her bed.

Hazel got on all fours and started toward the middle when she felt his weight on the bed. He grabbed her around the waist and pulled her so she was on just her knees, her back against his chest. The kissing never stopped. He could kiss her until she died. He was so goddamned good at it.

He had both hands on her breasts, sliding underneath her shirt but still on top of her bra. He used his thumbs on her nipples—just her nipples. She reached behind her to find a part of him to caress. The best she could do was his ass.

He paused to pull her shirt off. She had on a thin, pink bra. It was comfortable, but still cute, and then he had her locked against his chest, both still on their knees.

Her throat was dry. He had no intention of going faster. He flipped her onto her back, and she looked up at him from the bed. He knew how to manhandle a woman, and she tried not to be jealous of all the women that came before her.

He didn't give her time to do anything but feel, pulling the cups of her bra low so that her nipples were there for him. No words, just his hands. He fondled just her nipples for eternity. Thumbed them, pinched them, and added his teeth first to one and then the other.

She was writhing under him, and he kept blocking her from touching him.

Next was the full breast groping, interspersed with the nipple play. The buildup of heat between her legs for him was almost unbearable.

She was still half dressed. He still had on his shirt. And pants.

He might actually kill her.

"I want to see you. While you do this." She'd wanted to say it, but she panted it instead.

A little bit of a smirk brought out his dimple, and he pulled off his shirt for her.

He seemed to have a plan for her, but she stopped him with her palm. "Put your skin on mine."

The smirk dropped and the appreciation he regarded her with almost made her tear up.

She opened her arms to him.

XOXOXOXO

Wolf looked at her open arms and saw all that she was. Being asked to hold her was not something he deserved. Surely there were great guys out there who deserved to feel her.

Sex was one thing, but her energy was hitting him at a million miles an hour. It was staggering. She was letting him in.

He saw her fall in love with him. Right then, he watched a pink glow mix with her normal, goldish hue. He didn't feel worthy of her, but he couldn't say no.

He slowly climbed on top of her, and her arms came around him before rubbing his back.

He buried his face in her hair. Her energy surrounded him. And if he was inside of her, it might even fill him up.

There was contentment in her sigh. For a person like her, giving was how she received what mattered most.

He kissed her forehead. "Thank you for letting me in tonight."

She smiled, and his heart jumped off the cliff it had been standing on.

He needed her then; his plan to make her beg for him was abandoned. Wolf was desperate to get there before the energy shifted.

He stood from the bed and removed the rest of his clothes. Hazel started clapping, making him laugh. He tugged on her jeans, and she helped him wiggle them off of her. And then he had her on her bed, naked as she should be. It was better than he hoped it would be. And the door was locked. No one was going to walk in on them. He had her for as long as she would let him.

He ran a hand from her shoulder to her belly to her sex. Her pussy should be cast in gold and hung on a damn wall. It was art. She was obviously a regular waxer, which wasn't necessary, but damn if the thought of her making sure it was maintained made him even harder.

She bent her knees and spread her legs.

For him.

Wolf was presented with two very, very beautiful possibilities. To lick her or put himself in her. It was the selfish part of him, the part that wanted to see if her energy would be his as well if they were connected, that made the decisions for him.

Wolf almost forgot himself before digging in the pocket of his discarded pants for the condom he'd put there. She sat up, legs still spread to urge him on.

He smiled at her rush to feel what he wanted to feel, as well.

He got back on the bed and between her legs. He would have her under him first because he had to see her eyes when they were together in this dirty, beautiful way.

Wolf moved forward until he was lined up with the part of her that would change everything between them. They locked eyes as he slowly slid inside her.

She groaned, so involved in her passion that she was ready for all of him even though he hadn't even touched her pussy yet. She lifted her hips and insisted on adding to the rhythm he was slowly trying to create.

He saw white for a second and then she was clear again. He had no way to explain her energy, color-wise. But there was a personalization now. Her energy was clearly his.

Mine. Ours. This. Now.

She pulled him down so that he was lying on top of her. In the most mundane of the sex positions, she was heaven. He could kiss her lips and inhale the scent at the base of her neck that was uniquely her.

Sex was sin—in his head, in his balls—just like he imagined it was for every guy, everywhere. Until now. Until her. It was a connection so graceful and dazzling he realized she'd changed this thing for him. It went from a release to a foundation.

He slipped an arm under her. He had to have her come. He needed to see it. Needed to be a part of her body when she was so vulnerable. So he could have her pleasure.

Hazel knew. Somehow, she knew. Maybe it was as it should be. This sex was different. She ran her hands through his hair, down his face. She put her hand on his heart.

This was where they started.

Wolf slipped a hand between them, needing her panting more than his own breathing. The build was slow at first, and he witnessed a tempest in her eyes before she was forced to seal them shut. The moisture from her wet him, and it was all he needed to focus on his own release. She urged him on even in the throes of her own pleasure.

And when he came, it was into her. He got why men fought to protect a woman. He got why they would drive across country, why they would settle down.

It was her. She. Hazel was his to betray, to make proud, to hold.

It was overwhelming. He put his face against her shoulder as his last thrusts didn't bring a wave of the need to abandon as they had in the past. Instead of fear rushing in, her welcome became his home.

She hugged him then, kissed his temple like she loved him. She breathed her praise in his ear. Her thanks.

Wolf rolled to his side and pulled her in close, wrapping his arms around her, kissing her head, and then the tip of her nose and her lips.

His breaths were shaky. He loved her. It was far too soon, but he was the last person on the face of the earth to say that to anyone, considering he watched love at first sight happen on the regular. Hazel's skin was warm. He touched as much of it as he could.

"I shouldn't have let you leave my office before. But now, having had you here, in private, I'm glad. This was meant to be savored." He touched her nipple with his index finger and tried to decide what made it the most perfect one he'd ever seen. Or licked. Or sucked. The color? The perfect pucker?

Hazel was silent. She didn't say anything and she wasn't smiling. Wolf felt a flicker of fear light an ice fire at the base of his spine. Could he be wrong? Was what he'd just felt only one-sided? He couldn't be wrong. He was a goddamned savant when it came to this stuff.

And then she whispered, "Maybe you should go."

And This Is
When It Ends

Hazel knew she was in love with Wolf. It hit her in the heart so fatally, seeing him above her, giving her the most protective look ever, that she was on the verge of telling him.

But she remembered the last time she'd felt that way. The last time she'd uttered those words. She'd said them too soon. She'd said them on the tail end of an orgasm.

And now she knew she'd been wrong. What she'd felt for Scott was her desire to be in love.

What just happened with Wolf had made him a part of her soul. She swore she felt their futures touch. And she was petrified. Hazel had to get him out of her place before she screwed up. Before she told him what she was desperate to say. It was right on the tip of her tongue.

It was crazy how powerful the word was in this situation. How easily she could wound herself with it and scare him away.

At work, she said it all the time. She told her kids she loved them all the damn time.

Wolf was the love of her life. She knew that as clearly as she knew her name. If she were a matchmaker, she would bet on him and her.

So when she asked him to leave, it was her last chance at self-protection. She watched him close his eyes for a moment. His jaw tensed and he shook his head the tiniest bit. He swallowed. In her throat, the words she wanted to say were stuck on the flypaper of her past experience. It was like watching him lose a belief—seeing the disappointment hit him.

While Wolf got up and put his clothes on, he seemed to start and stop an argument four different times. "You know what, Hazel? Be safe. Be good. I wish you happiness." He gave her a little bow and walked out of her bedroom.

She changed her mind and ran after him just as the front door closed. By the time she got her robe around her and out to the hall, the elevator was already showing it was on the first floor.

Hazel came back inside and closed her door softly, before leaning against it. Maybe it was a self-fulfilling prophecy, this feeling. It was as if her heart had been torn from its moorings.

Should have just told him. Taken another risk. Pain is just pain anyway, and she was already hurting.

XOXOXOXO

Hazel wanted another chance. She wanted Wolf to come back so she could say better things to him. Let him know that she felt like the most important decision of her life was careening off the road, and she couldn't stop it. And she wanted to stop it.

When she talked to Claire the next morning, her best friend gave her the news before the bus full of her kids rolled in. Wolf had pushed on to the next stop on the tour because he wanted to lock in the new venue. Hazel was grateful for her full plate at school so she only had small respites of longing for him.

According to Claire, he was gone. He'd texted Chance that he was maybe looking up an old girlfriend. And that was that. Hazel thought at least she would see him at Claire and Chance's wedding, but even that was up for grabs. Chance had even picked out a substitute best man. And maybe if Wolf did come he would have a date already.

Chance was stressed as he tried to plan the Booty Camp success reunion for a few hours before the rehearsal dinner in the theater while Claire made the last-minute adjustments for their big day.

Hazel threw herself into elaborate lesson plans and redesigned her brag board with the kids' achievements in the hall outside her classroom twice. Claire seemed concerned, but Hazel put her acting to use—her best friend needed to spend time with her man. Eating food delivered to the school for dinner, Hazel was able to reorganize the kids' desks and reorder all her sensory activities according to color and preference. There was always work to do in a classroom. And after everyone had left—save for the maintenance crew who always seemed to be running a loud machine—she could cry.

She hated on Wolf's new girl—who ever she was. And time passed. Days turned into a week and then it was time to face Claire and Chance's happily ever after.

In an effort to be a good friend, Hazel had helped address invites and even pitched in with Chance and Booty Camp's last soirée.

On the evening of the rehearsal dinner, Hazel was the point person for the rehearsal decorations as the Booty Camp team cleaned up after the success party. She had baby pictures of Chance and Claire to post and family members to welcome. Luckily, the theater was available for the two-hour party.

She had on her long black dress with the thin straps and had straightened her hair for a change from her loose waves.

She used flowers and some fun decorations to change the atmosphere while Chance worked on last-minute Booty Camp details in his office.

When Chance came out to see how she was doing since he'd let her in with an armload of bags, he was very pleased. He looked tired, though, and she told him as much.

He rubbed his eyes. "I would love a little sleep, but that'll come eventually. Now, it's important I make sure Claire has a wedding to remember. I don't want the rush to take away how special it should be for her."

Hazel patted Chance's shoulder. "I think you can't help but make her happy. Hang in there."

Chance pulled out his phone. "Oh shit. I forgot to check with this supplier. I'll be right back. People should be arriving soon. Thank you so much, Hazel. You're really a wedding planning powerhouse."

She didn't tell him that organizing things were a teacher's strong suit. She added a few more flowers to the sconce lights when she heard the front door open.

It was Wolf.

He was dressed up, and her throat went dry. Wolf in a suit was exactly what Hazel would forever use in her mind's eye to describe the word sexy.

He met her eyes as if he was expecting her.

There was no other woman with him. And she was grateful.

She was ready for the fighting. Instantly, like his presence reared up her fire. But he crossed the distance to her and put his hand on her lower back, giving her a cheek kiss he would lay on a great aunt.

"Hazel. You look lovely. Nice to see you." He inclined his head in her direction. "Is Chance around?" he asked as though he'd never tasted her vagina even once.

Two could play at the unaffected game. "He's in his office. Nice seeing you, as well."

She turned away from him before he had a chance to block her out first.

As soon as Wolf went into the office she rushed to her purse to text Claire. But then she stopped. This wasn't the night to drag her friend into her drama. The woman was meeting her in-laws, introducing her parents... she needed only peace and helpfulness from Hazel.

So she packed up the rest of the boxes and started tucking them out of sight. She didn't want to interrupt Chance and Wolf, so she went to Wolf's office to slide the boxes away.

Her energy told her he was behind her before her traditional senses noticed. It was dazzling. Then super depressing.

He knocked lightly on his own door.

This was not the man who'd stalked her and claimed her mouth in the past. He was polite. Distant. Like she meant nothing special to him at all.

"Chance mentioned you helped with planning the soirée, so I just wanted to offer you compensation for your time." He pulled out his wallet. "I was helping a friend. Not everything is about money."

She felt a chill on her shoulders.

"Of course, but legally it's better if I make sure everyone who works at Booty Camp is adequately reimbursed for their time and energy." He started to count the bills in his wallet between his index finger and thumb.

She was done pretending. "Really, Wolf? This is how it is for you? You're trying to *pay* me? Should I ask how much I earned when I gargled your dick upside-down on that desk?"

His eyes went wide, and he quickly shut the door. "Jesus, Hazel."

"Sorry, was I not supposed to mention that service? Or was that part okay to administer to a friend for free?" Hazel put her hands on her hips.

Wolf bit his lips together before looking at her. "I don't know what to make of you. I honestly don't. What do you want, Hazel?"

And she didn't want to tell him. That was pointless and seemed desperate right now. She didn't want to tell him that she was crazy about him. That he infuriated her to the point of breaking, but his lips were the most tempting thing she'd ever seen. Still. That she wished he could see through her enough to not need her to speak it. Because she wanted at least a little pride at the end of this whole show. And God knew where this old girlfriend he was looking up was. That burned.

"Not you," she lied. She lied to protect her heart and watched him crumple a little.

He put his hand on the back of his neck, rubbing it. "I got that when you kicked me out last time. Have great sex and then tell me to leave. That's what Scott taught you, and you're teaching me, I guess."

She realized he was right. Except that she'd told Scott she loved him and Wolf had done no such thing. But still. She hadn't looked at it that way.

She was quieter now, less furious. "I didn't intend to do that to you. I was scared. I was afraid that it felt too good with you."

"Well, that's a hard thing to read in a mind." Wolf wasn't any softer, and his glare had an edge. "If I was able to do that."

"If you could have read my mind it would have been even scarier." She plucked at an invisible thread on her dress, avoiding the eye contact. She could hear the crowd starting to arrive for the rehearsal party through the office door.

When she looked up, his face was tender again. It was like pouring vinegar on a burn. It hurt less when he was distant.

"What would I have seen in your head, Hazel?" God he was impressive.

It was worse knowing what he did to her. How he'd looked at her the last time they were naked.

She shook her head, refusing to allow him that access.

He stepped closer. "Can I tell you what I was thinking?"

He held out his hand as if for a handshake. She was wary.

227

Was this when he told her that the dates had been nice, but he shook her hand like a friend?

She had no other choice now that he was being nice. She gripped his hand like they were on their best manners and being introduced for the first time. Hazel didn't give him permission, but when he covered her hand with his other one, her heart was pounding out of her chest.

Even closer. "Can I?"

She nodded her head once, allowing him to open this gate to her hopes one last time.

Wolf changed his grip and brought her hand to his mouth, placing a kiss on her knuckles, before moving in on her more and touching her forehead with his own.

"I was thinking you were amazing. I was thinking that I knew the difference between fucking and making love."

She inhaled sharply with his use of the filthy word.

"I was wondering if this was how it felt for people to be matched by me." He nudged her face toward him with his nose and spoke his next words against her lips. "To fall so crazy in love that everything that mattered was right in front of me."

Like a shot of lightening in her psyche, she was forced to look at him, had to see his mouth so she knew her head wasn't lying to her.

His eyes crinkled at the corners. "I've counted myself out for so long that falling in love with you almost hurt. I tried to screw it up so many times because I'm such a dick. And then I had you. I felt you. I knew this was it. We were it. My future got started right there, in your bed. Hell, it started when I laid eyes on you, but I was too much of a dick to know better."

He stepped backward then, kissing her hand again before letting it go. She covered her mouth with the hand he'd released.

"You asked me to leave, and I doubted everything I knew to be true. I needed space away from you. I couldn't see our severed future in your beautiful face. But I missed you. And that's what I was thinking."

She spoke but kept her hand over her mouth a little, frightened of what she asked next. "What are you thinking now?"

His wry grin showed a hint of his dimple. "That you are more gorgeous than I remembered. Which seems impossible, yet here you are. That I can't do this again. I can't fall so hard ever again. I won't be able to think straight. I can't make matches. I won't. That I can be giving all these people this kind of pain if their match turns them away? It's torture."

He shoved his hands in the pockets of his suit pants. "And this is my lot. Because I messed with the system. My mother and grandmother were right. I'm reaping what I've sown by monetizing the family talent." Wolf shrugged.

Hazel let his words filter through all the walls she'd erected and scars she'd acquired. She realized he'd told her his deepest fear. The teacher in her processed that first. She could fix that. She could reassure him.

"They're wrong." She watched him search her face. "You're a force of love, and that's not wrong. Claire met the love of her life here. God, how many matches have I seen? Connecting that kind of positivity is powerful. Sometimes change is hard for elders but utilizing technology to help people find love makes sense. Love is never wrong. I think I understand their superstitions because it must be hard to see things evolve rapidly in just one generation. I think you're entitled to an endless fountain of beauty. You're not cursed. I don't believe that." She stepped across the room and touched his face while he held his breath. "I'm so crazy in love with you, and I'm terrified."

His eyes widened and then focused. "What?"

"I love you." Hazel felt like she was falling backward off a sheer cliff. It sounded insane. It felt like a roller coaster. "I know that you've moved on. Claire told me about you looking up an old girlfriend..." She wanted to wish him love and joy but her tongue refused to play nice. Instead she just trailed off.

He half smiled while confusion lifted one of his eyebrows. It was like a light bulb went off above him when it clicked. "Oh! I told Chance that so he wouldn't come to find me. That's Chance's thing. He makes sure I'm not self-destructing." Wolf shrugged as his smile completed itself. "I'm betting he told Claire who told you."

"So there's no new lady?" Hazel clapped her hands in front of her and then touched her fingertips to her lips in anticipation of his answer. This could change everything.

"There's only you." Wolf slid closer to her, his white teeth blinding when he beamed. "And you love me. So, I'm not cursed?"

Hazel laughed. "Well, some might say falling for me is a horrible curse."

"We're saying this? We're allowed to say this?" He took his

hands out of his pockets, ran them up her sides, and wrapped his arms around her.

"I think so. I think we did." Hazel ran her thumbs over his lips before placing a kiss there. "I love you, Wolf."

"You're mine?" Wolf kissed her so much she couldn't answer so she just nodded, affirming it for him.

She felt a few tears start to fall. Her hands were actually shaking she was so open and scared.

He caught them up and kissed them when he noticed they were trembling. "Don't. Don't be scared. We can do this. I'll make it work."

"I believe you."

Trusting him was like watching a mystery revealed. Everything clicked, and finally her rational mind agreed with her heart.

"We're *us* now." He kissed her more, holding her hands between them like they were making a promise. With his delighted smile, her forever began.

Maid Of Honor
And Best Man

The kissing and embracing went on far longer than it should've considering Hazel was the maid of honor and Wolf was the best man at the rehearsal party on the opposite side of the door.

Hazel was in love with Wolf, but even better, acknowledging their feelings finally allowed them to be friends.

"So, obviously, we have to be cordial and not kissing out there." Hazel pointed at the door they had to go through soon.

He ignored her and kissed her some more. When she was finally able to turn her head, she laughed. "I'm in love with a man named Wolf. Who would have ever thought?"

He tickled her. "You'll learn to love it. It's really rare. Why can't we keep kissing?"

Hazel shimmied away from his hands but couldn't get away. "There are a lot of your employees at that party, remember? Are you going to be at the wedding tomorrow?"

He nuzzled her neck, answering against her skin, "Yes, I'm going. No, the employees can't see me dry humping you."

When his mouth moved to her chest and he added the tip of his tongue, she pushed him away. "Some of them might have seen us come in here. We might even have to be frigid to one another."

He bit her gently. "No way. I can't possibly keep my hands off you, and I'm never treating you like that again."

That made her smile, and he kissed her again the minute she did.

"I may have to change the rules. To tell my people they can't have this—it's not fair." Wolf touched her face with his fingertips. "Come on. We're going out there." He took her hand and kissed it again. She expected him to drop it the minute they exited, but instead, he hung tight.

Hazel felt herself blush as she watched the guests who knew her or Wolf or both take in the fact that they were very couple-y.

XOXOXOXO

Wolf met each pair of eyes he found pinned on him and Hazel. Instead of judgment, anger, or scorn, his employees smiled and raised a glass. He wordlessly acknowledged them.

Wolf found Claire and Chance standing in the center of the lobby, holding court. When Chance saw Hazel and Wolf walking toward him hand-in-hand, he was delighted.

He bent low and whispered to Claire. Claire scanned the crowd and found them. Her jaw dropped.

For her benefit, Wolf stopped, turned to Hazel, and pulled her into a kiss.

Hazel's mouth was the distraction it would always be, and it took the applause a second to register in his consciousness.

When he turned to look back at their best friends, they were clapping the loudest.

Hazel looped her arm in his and rose up on her tiptoes. He leaned down to hear her thoughtful concern. "I don't want to take their spotlight."

He kissed her forehead. "Okay. But don't worry. It's cool."

He felt like he was four hundred feet tall and bulletproof. He'd found her, and they'd communicated despite themselves. He wouldn't be a matchless matchmaker forever. She thought he was good luck, not bad.

This was the best night of his life.

He gave Chance the handshake they always had for each other and slapped him on his huge back.

Claire enveloped Hazel in a girl grab full of knowing looks and gossip.

Chance started the conversation. "Proud of you, man. 'Bout damn time. You could cut the sexual tension between you two with a frigging knife."

Wolf thanked the server who handed him his rum on the rocks. "Yeah. She's the one."

Chance punched Wolf in the arm. "The one? Like, forever?"

Wolf took a sip, watching as Claire and Hazel had what seemed like a very similar discussion.

"Brother. This is a big night. And a big gesture, if you know what I mean." Chance indicated the party, where at least forty percent of his staff was in attendance.

"I do. And I think it might be time for an employee handbook update. I think if I can tell that the employee has met their match, they should be allowed to pursue it. I mean it can't be an all-out orgy or anything."

Wolf took another sip while Chance supplied the "Damn it."

He chuckled. "But it's not fair to deny them this just because they have the misfortune to work for me."

Chance held up his glass. "It's never a misfortune. It's a great opportunity. But I'm willing to bet all of your chest hair that you'll be much more fun now that you won't be a grumpy blue ball owner all the damn time."

Wolf gave Chance the middle finger by scratching his forehead with it and razzed him back. "I heard you get less sex after you get the ol' ball and chain installed."

Wolf didn't hear the response from his friend because Hazel was smiling at him and time stopped. She was his. She was stunning. And he was going to screw the hell out of her as soon as he could tonight. Or sooner.

XⓞXⓞXⓞXⓞ

The party was amazing. Having Wolf as her date made her feel like a million dollars. She lost count of the female employees who'd accosted her in the bathroom the two times she went and the few who'd caught her walking to and from. They wanted to know if the rules had changed. As it turned out, quite a few girls had a thing for another employee or had had to walk away from a past client that they had feelings for.

Hazel wished them luck and recommended that they speak to Wolf. Maybe her relationship with him would lead to more matches within the company.

He was so attentive. To look in his direction and know that she would be welcome in his gaze was addicting. She was stupid about it. He kept finding ways to come near her and kiss her cheek or touch her lower back as he mingled. Throughout the party, it was a wonderful build up.

They helped Chance and Claire clean up and lock up on the way out. Hazel changed into the casual outfit she brought with her. The wedding was in just over a week. Wolf hailed a cab for them, and Hazel didn't question it. He gave an address she didn't recognize, and in just a few minutes, they were pulling up to an elegant brownstone. He paid the cab and led Hazel to the door, touching her as often as possible.

Being with him was a relief, really. It was like her heart knew they were supposed to be like this and her head and the circumstances had finally caught up.

Wolf took her wrap and hung it in the closet as Hazel got her first glance at the place he'd called home while Booty Camp was in town.

"Rented?" It seemed like the obvious solution to his housing needs.

"Yeah. Everything in here is rented. The place came furnished." Wolf held out his arms, and she walked into his embrace.

"Does that feel unwelcoming? Is it like this for every city?" She put her head on his chest.

"Yeah. I bring a box of my stuff and scatter it around so I have reminders of home. You want some more wine?" He ran his hands up and down her arms.

"Oh yes." He left her to go into the kitchen and open a bottle. Hazel started to nose around, seeing if she could pick out the things that were actually his.

And then she spied a picture that stopped her cold. It was a picture of her from when she was a little kid.

"What the hell?" She grabbed the frame from the bookcase where it sat next to a clear packet of dried flowers.

Wolf walked over with two wineglasses and set them on the coffee table, looking puzzled.

He took the frame and gave her a wary look. "This is my sister."

Hazel was shocked. "Faith is your sister?"

The look on his face matched the puzzlement she felt. "My sister's name was Faith."

"I remember that you told me that now. Did she go to the Girl Scout camp at Camp Fortnight?" Hazel stood next to him so they could both look at the picture.

He frowned. "I don't remember."

Hazel felt tears crowd her eyes as she took the picture from his hands. "Who is this?" She pointed to the little brunette Faith had her arm around. The girls were smiling and looking at each other.

Wolf again had no answer. But it was okay because Hazel did.

"This is my friend, Faith. That's me in this picture. I went away to camp when I was six, and I was having trouble with being homesick and making friends. Faith was a camper there. She was so kind to me. She and I would draw horses together in art. Faith always had time for me."

237

DEBRA ANASTASIA

Hazel let the tears fall then. "But your sister passed away? That's what you said before."

Wolf took the picture back and looked harder. "It is you. Holy crap. It's you. How is this possible?"

"Because my dad was military—we moved a lot. We weren't even in your state six months. Faith's the reason I decided to become a special education teacher. I loved getting to know her. I have a very similar picture of she and I on my desk at work." Hazel wiped her tears away.

Wolf's eyes clouded. "This is a picture of you and my sister."

Hazel sat on the couch and pulled him to sit next to her.

"I'm so sorry she's gone." Hazel felt the loss on the adult level, but the little girl in her did, too.

"Me, too. All day. Every day. But you know why. You loved her, too." Wolf put his arm around her shoulders.

"I can't tell you how much she meant to me that summer. I felt so safe because she was a little older than me." Hazel touched the picture of Faith.

"She had a knack for that. For making people feel wanted. At home. She was so incredible." Wolf kissed Hazel's temple.

"I wish she was here." Hazel gasped with the start of the full-out sobbing. Because the sureness of the coincidence was hitting her all at once.

Wolf turned to face her and held her face. "Don't you see? She is. She's right here. This is her way of telling me she loved you first." Hazel had no shame about her emotion as she curled into his chest. "How many kids have you helped because you knew Faith?"

He tilted their hug a bit so he could reach the tissues. He

238

wiped her tears away. "Oh God. A lot. I hope. I mean, that's the reason I go to work in the morning, but this job can feel like ten steps backward for every step forward. But I hope I've helped."

"I'm always amazed how many people she affected, but this feels like a visit from her, almost. It's so crazy." Wolf patted her back.

She looked up at him and had to wipe two tears from his cheeks, as well.

They spent the rest of the evening on the couch. The bottle of wine migrated from the kitchen to the living room as they shared stories.

Wolf told her about Faith. Funny stories, stories that broke her heart. The tale of his sister's last beautiful moment on earth—too soon but full of her endless optimism as Faith comforted their mother and grandmother and him before she was done adding her light to their lives.

Hazel told him about her childhood. She shared stories about her kids, telling him about each one.

At the start of her night, Hazel thought for sure she would be enjoying much more carnal pleasures with this ridiculously hot guy. But seeing him as he truly was, who he was, was sexy, too. They had so much to learn about each other. They were exhausted by the time the dawn started to heat up the night, and curling up on the couch seemed about right. Before Hazel drifted off to sleep on his chest, she looked at the picture one last time.

Faith and Hazel a million years ago. Friends.

M♡RNING LiGhT

Knowing Hazel was right for him changed how his eyes focused in the morning light. A wave of emotion hit him as the sight of her in his arms. Undeniable. His fate had been headed for hers all this time.

Which would sound like a cheesy romance novel if that very thing wasn't the business he traded in. But to be on the receiving end of that service? Now he had a deeper understanding of why his company was so successful.

And her. This new revelation that he wasn't doomed to be unfulfilled by love was a game changer. That she could be right, maybe there was happiness headed his way. If his heart didn't feel like a superhero right now, he wouldn't believe it was possible.

He rubbed her brown hair between his fingers.

Hazel. The girl of his dreams was named Hazel. And he thanked the fates and energies that continued to put her in front of him until they clicked.

She moaned a little and snuggled in deeper to his chest.

Judging from the height of the shadows and the pure white of the sunshine peeking under the blinds, it was early.

Maybe they had been asleep three hours, tops.

Her loose fist on his chest slowly splayed out as she woke. "Wolf?"

"It's me." He ran his knuckles down her arm.

"Oh good. I thought you were a dream. I was scared." She laughed a little as she shifted.

"Don't be. I'm here now." She was lovely. Beyond pretty. Just the glow her energy put on her skin—it radiated the beauty he should have been seeking his whole life.

She looked up at him. "Lucky me. Does it feel weird that we're not fighting?"

He started laughing. "A little. I like this a whole lot better, though."

Wolf kissed her forehead, and she pushed up until she was able to straddle him. "Same."

He was grateful they'd talked all night because now he could have her in new daylight. He wanted to see it all. Feel her. See her.

She leaned down and kissed his lips. How did he get so lucky? With her hands, she demanded he take off his shirt completely. It had been hanging open when they fell asleep. Her hair tickled his chest and shoulders when she came in for more kisses.

Wolf couldn't put into words how she made him feel, so he didn't. He showed her.

XOXOXOXO

Hazel had felt fear leave her after seeing the picture of Faith.

Which was probably premature when it came to her

feelings about Wolf, but it made sense in the sweetest of ways. When Hazel was in camp as a kid, it had been a quick stopover for her military family. It had been a tough time, and at just six, she'd been more introverted than she ever had in her life.

When she'd gone to the art special, there was a different class with her age group. They were a year or so older. Faith had picked the empty space next to Hazel, and when she'd looked at the girl, her smile was a welcome comfort on a scary day.

Sometimes Faith was hard to understand, but it was okay because they liked to draw horses together. When there were camp-wide lunches, Hazel would find Faith and sit next to her.

Faith was always happy to see Hazel and made her feel like she was the best part of Faith's day.

During the time Hazel spent at the camp, she watched the counselors, who were much older than the teenage girls in charge of her group. She liked how they spoke to the children. She liked how encouraging they were, and even though a lot of the kids in Hazel's group were different than the people she'd met before, they were all comfortable with themselves.

When it had been time to leave summer camp, Hazel cried. She'd wanted to spend more time with Faith during art. Her parents had taken a picture of the girls together, and Faith made Hazel laugh the instant the shutter captured the moment.

The picture on Wolf's coffee table was taken on a different day. Faith's counselors must have snapped it when they weren't looking.

As Hazel grew older, she never forgot Faith or the way her counselors treated the kids that summer. So when it was time to start to pick a career path, Hazel knew which one she wanted to take.

When people praised her for the job she did, Hazel usually accepted it with as much grace as she could at the time. But she knew the kids were a gift. Would always be a gift. They gave so much more than they took. Hazel learned that from Faith. And that same spark was something she got to see in Jonah and Kenzie and all her other kids every day she taught.

But Wolf knew that secret. He was Faith's brother. There was no way he could have missed out on being put under Faith's spell of kindness and positivity.

"What are you thinking about?" Wolf tucked a lock of her hair behind her ear.

"Faith." Hazel leaned into his hand.

Wolf bowed his head briefly.

"Just how people don't always know that we're the lucky ones. Because we got to know her." Hazel turned her head and kissed his palm.

"You are exceptional. Being who you are. It suits you." Wolf watched her lips on his hand.

"Do you have a nice bedroom? I want to see the Wolf's lair." She got off his lap.

He groaned as he got off the couch. "That was a long time to be crammed on that sucker."

He took her hand and led her upstairs.

Wolf's bedroom in the rental house was very neutral, but wonderful. She liked seeing where he let his guard down at the end of a day in her city.

Hazel loved that it was time to be with him this way.

He was undressed first, and she spun in time to see the main event. His dick was a thing of beauty. It was long enough to make her clench internally and thick enough to make her sigh.

"Everything okay?"

She smiled. His presence delivered a sexual punch that screamed of the pleasure he would bring her. Here.

"Can you wear less, too?" Wolf approached her and started on her shirt. They'd been together for hours and hours and she still had her shirt on. It made taking it off even more intimate.

He set it sweetly on his chair. Like he planned to put it back on her when they were done. Then he did the same with her jeans. Her shoes had been left at the door.

Wolf grinned at her. "Best view in the whole city right now."

He skimmed her shape with his hands. She caught them and stepped into the hug she'd made him create for her.

Wolf ran his fingers up her spine and lightly traced back down. Then he grabbed her ass hard enough for her to yelp. She covered his hands with her own.

His hardness was pressed against her belly. She looked down at the smooth tip. It was really a pretty dick. Lucky her.

He slipped his hands under her bra and found her nipples. He strummed her with them, making her moan. They were standing up for him, and his hands had a slight chill, which increased the feelings.

She snaked her hand between them so she could stroke

him. It made him arch against her.

"Your hands…"

She used them both now that she had him off balance, twisting her grip gently to send a variation of sensations through him.

He let her do it for a few seconds, hissing when she ran her thumb over the tip and felt the wetness there. She bit her lip, feeling powerful.

His eyes flashed at the gloating in her expression, and he retaliated with his own seeking hands.

He went to the front of her panties with one hand and the back with the other. Wolf's fingers became all she could focus on. He filled her in every place that would make her knees weak. The rubbing, mixed with the pumping of his knowledgeable fingers, was like riding a rocket to her orgasm.

She was losing balance. He bent down and bit her nipple as he found her clit again and again and applied the perfect pressure that made it feel like she was on the edge of pain.

He added more fingers so that she had so many inside. More than she could take, almost. He was just getting her ready.

When he went to his knees and put his mouth directly on her, she shouted.

He hummed and licked and sucked until she had to put her hands on his shoulders to stay upright.

"I can't… I can't…"

She couldn't articulate that she was going to fall. Everything inside her was on an edge that he owned. He understood, and for that she was grateful. He nudged her backwards and helped her stay steady until she was backed up to his bed.

He stood and took away all her favorite toys, which happened to be his hands, and used them to toss her in the center of the bed.

After pulling off her panties and wrestling her out of her bra, he had to hold her down so she would stop trying to rush him to make him be inside her, or so that she could put her mouth on him instead.

"Stop. Your pussy is my favorite meal."

She couldn't argue with logic like that, so she waited with wild anticipation for him to return to her.

Then he was between her legs, inserting his fingers and being creative with his lips and tongue. She would take breaks from the white only he made her see to catch sight of him. His back muscles working, his sharp jaw running against her thigh, his fingers moving in and out of her.

She was so close; the release was going to possibly stop her heart because it was building in her chest with the same ferocity as it was between her legs.

She pushed him away-- surprised at her own strength.

"I want to come on your dick." Hazel swirled her hips while he watched. His eyes rolled back in his head, and he groaned.

"Oh fuck."

Wolf spoke against her lips. "I need to put on a condom."

He reached past her to the nightstand drawer and pulled out the recognizable package for his package. He kneeled so he could slide it on, and she felt another spark of lust as she watched him touch himself.

Wolf moved closer and closer until he was lined up. When he was finally sliding in, she matched him, not letting him choose a slower pace.

Hazel knew they only had a small window of actual screwing because they were both close. She raised her hips to meet him and every time he topped out inside her, he hit a perfect spot that was dragging a new level of orgasm out of her.

He pulled out when she was *this* close, and she was actually angry when he denied her his dick.

Wolf growled and went back into his nightstand. He grabbed two nipple clamps.

"Ever used these?"

"No. But I want to use whatever you want to use."

He had pinched her nipple enough that he could adjust the clamp to his liking. She yipped. The dastardly grin on his face made her overact to the next clamp a bit.

Wolf was grinding in her. He was a goddamned genius. He thumbed her clit over and over and over while hitting that delicious spot. The clips were the most beautiful horrible.

She was grinding hard against him, begging him to make it happen, whatever *it* was going to be.

"Look at me," he demanded, and she did as he directed. He never stopped on her clit as he released the clamps, the rush of blood to both of her nipples brought her orgasm through her like a hurricane in a tornado.

She certainly came on his dick. While she was in the throes of her own personal resurrection, she felt him tense and watched as the veins in his arms thickened.

He came hard, continuing thrust after thrust as she

wrapped her ankles around his ass so she could squeeze every last bit of lust out of him.

He collapsed on top of her, and she hugged him, kissing his forehead. "Thank you so much."

"No, thank you." Wolf adjusted her so she was on his biceps, and that was the last thing she remembered before they fell asleep together.

WEddiNGS

There were four condoms in the trash in his room and a pile of wet towels. For Wolf the rest of the day was flashes.

Hazel naked, laughing at a joke he'd told.

Hazel wet and soapy, pressed against his shower door.

Hazel on her hands and knees, tossing her hair over her shoulder to look back at him.

It was glorious. They eventually realized they had to eat. Come up for air. He'd put his pants on to make her eggs and toast. And like an angel from heaven, she'd stayed naked for the whole process.

She ate at his kitchen island. It might have been dinnertime. It didn't matter. She was with him.

Their phones alerted them to a ton of missed notifications.

She walked their plates to the sink, and he couldn't take his eyes off her.

"You're the best man and I'm the maid of honor in a wedding next week. We may have to check our phones." She wiggled her cute ass over to the couch, and he couldn't help but stop her with his hands on her breasts, pulling her to his chest as he trapped her.

"Again? Already?" She didn't sound disappointed.

When he bent her over the arm of the couch, he had the awe-inspiring view of her glorious ass, and she was ready for him. He made sure she had the imprint of the couch material on her skin after he thrust into her over and over. Then he let her look at her phone. "Uh. Claire is freaking out." She laughed a little and patted the seat next to her on the couch.

She turned the camera to face them and snapped a selfie of them with their heads together.

He watched as she typed.

Be there soon. Ran into a Wolf. Naked.

He kissed her cheek and then decided her ears were his favorite curl ever.

Claire's response came quickly.

Get it, girl.

After some back and forth, Hazel promised to meet Claire in Fancy Pants at 6:30 p.m. Which was in about an hour. She sent a message that Wolf was coming with them, so Claire told them to ignore the messages from Chance. They were due to pick up the suits, as well.

Wolf didn't want to leave. Stepping back into the world gave them responsibilities and time apart. Here they were in the bubble of being in love, and he was addicted to it already.

Chance was smart. He'd figured out immediately what it had taken Wolf six weeks to learn. Never give up on love.

It was going to be okay, he was sure of it. No matter the trials the travel schedule put on them, Wolf knew that he and Hazel would be together in the future. His sister had put her seal of approval on the relationship all those years ago.

Together they got dressed and gathered her things. They took a cab over to the shop and were immediately razzed for being late and being together.

Peter looked disappointed, and that just made Wolf want to nail Hazel one more time in front of him. But that wasn't the way it was going to go. Chance had gotten him on the side to confirm that Scott was happily dating his deserving match. Wolf shared a handshake with Chance as he pictured Scott with the girl who had such a similar, dickheaded energy spiraling into the relationship they both deserved.

When Claire and Hazel had left the guys to go to their part of the store for one final fitting, Peter sidled up to Wolf.

"So I've been hearing rumors about getting to date clients. Hazel change that for you?" The tall guy folded himself into a plush chair.

"Maybe," Wolf answered. He wanted to protect how strong his feelings for Hazel were right now. "But the important part is that if I can find your redheaded ass a match, you'll be allowed to try and date her. Remember, I can't work miracles."

The truth was that Peter wouldn't need any miracles to seal the deal when he was ready. But he liked to tease the guy.

The suits fit, and the dressing rooms had been reinforced with actual wood, so Wolf's own wood was sad. He smiled when he heard Hazel tap on the other side as his phone pinged with a message from her.

I'm sad about this new wall.

My dick is also sad.

He silently thanked the world when a topless picture of Hazel came through on his phone.

Let the sexting begin...

XӨXӨXӨXӨ

On the wedding day, the ceremony between Chance and Claire was very personal. Wolf watched Hazel's eyes soften at the officiant's time-honored words. It was crazy that they'd simply had to let it happen. The love they felt. When they were able to stop sabotaging themselves, the future had been already laid out.

The night went on and Wolf got to have a short dance with the bride before spending the rest of the night with Hazel.

He wanted to spoil her and buy her jewelry, but nothing could shine brighter than the happiness on her face.

Booty Camp had claimed its latest success story, and Hazel and Wolf were well on their way to being another one.

They danced to the soft music long after everyone had seen Claire and Chance off on their honeymoon.

Wolf rested his cheek on her hair while Hazel hummed. "What're you thinking about?"

He felt her warm exhale on the side of his neck. "Your

mom and grandma."

Wolf backed up a smidge to look at her face with curiosity. "Why is that?"

"Last night on FaceTime, they seemed so happy. I think we need to pay them a real visit. It must be hard for them, thinking all this time you might not have a partner in life because of a talent they passed on to you." Hazel put her hand on his cheek and gave him a soft expression.

In his office weeks ago, Claire had told him that being loved by Hazel was life-altering. How right she was. Hazel loved him with her whole being. She thought about him, touched him and cuddled him in such a tender yet strong way that he was excited about their future. Both his mom and grandma had signed the email to him right after the FaceTime session had ended. They wrote that Hazel was his perfect match. The best one they had ever seen.

He turned his head so he could place a kiss on her palm before responding, "I never thought of it that way. I know it would concern me with any kid we have."

She dropped her gaze at his mention of their future child while her smile added rose to her cheeks.

His forever was in front of him. His energy and hers would create a beautiful bundle between them. And this would be his view of her as she looked down at their someday-baby.

"God, I'm so in love with you." He murmured.

She stopped dancing to hold his face and kiss him before telling him, "We're really going to be okay."

Wolf accepted this. He was 110% satisfied that they would be.

The End

Don't miss the Booty Camp Infomercials and #Grelp and
#Spacebook reviews on the Booty Camp website:
http://debraanastasia.wixsite.com/bootycampdating

Ab♥ut Debra:

Debra writes stories mostly in her pajamas with her hairy co-workers (dogs and a cat) to keep her company. Comedy, New Adult, Paranormal and Angst stories fill up her hard drive. A lot of her time is spent in the mom carpool lane. Debra has been married for 19 years to her favorite guy. She loves to laugh at her own farts in the morning and can be found on Facebook and Twitter being an idiot. She'll hug you if she ever meets you and will most likely smell like cotton candy when she does it.

Find her at DebraAnastasia.com

Can't get enough of Booty Camp Dating Service and the whole Booty team? Check out the custom website with tons of reviews as if it was a real company here: http://debraanastasia.wixsite.com/bootycampdating

It's hilarious and even has an infomercial section!

Want more laughter?

Read the first three chapters of the romantic comedy FIRE DOWN BELOW that is out NOW and enrolled in Kindle Unlimited:

Chapter 1

Keep Cold!

Dove clutched her second prescription in one week to her chest as she approached the pharmacy counter in Save-Mart. She hated getting any embarrassing drug filled. Specifically, medicines required for parts of her body below her belly button and above her knees.

She even tried ordering personal items online. Her tampons and maxi pads had arrived in a covert brown box on her doorstep. She didn't even have to look at the UPS deliveryman. Dove had peeked from behind the curtains in her apartment and waited until he was gone before she picked up the package. But her period was unpredictable and she was forgetful, so she had to do the period walk of shame damn near every month. Chocolate, something salty, and a box of hag rags gave her away to any cashier.

Her first UTI had snuck up on her like a hairy little kitten. She never got urinary tract infections, but when she wound up crying from the burning sensation while peeing, she made an appointment with her decidedly female general practitioner. Dove filled her prescription for antibiotics at her friendly Save-Mart pharmacy, comfortingly staffed by discreet ladies. Dove vaguely remembered commenting on her pharmacist's large belly. Mrs. Pills should be about eight and a half months pregnant as of right now.

When Dove found herself battling a yeast infection due to the powerful antibiotics, she had to make a return trip to her doctor and picked up her current prescription. Now, as she got to the

Save-Mart Pharmacy counter again, she waited patiently. She didn't see Mrs. Pills. From the conversation Dove overheard between the woman's assistants, she was now both a pharmacist and a happy mom to a healthy baby girl.

Dove didn't notice the gentleman tucking purple and white bags into uniform alphabetic rows until he noticed her first. She had no time to run with her prescription clearly in view. He unfurled his large frame and his handsome smile at the same time.

Oh crap, kill me. Someone kill me dead. A lot.

"Hello. Dropping off?"

His voice should have been counting down the hits on some radio station. His green eyes flashed with friendliness and maybe a bit of flirtation. Dove swallowed hard and nodded.

After an awkward pause, Mr. Fitzwell, as his nametag claimed, reached between her breasts to pluck the paper from her clenched hands. He raised an inquisitive eyebrow—possibly at her bizarre behavior—and smoothed the paper on the laminate counter. Dove wanted to crap her pants when he announced the name of her drug way louder than Mrs. Pills would ever mention a lady prescription.

"Gynazule®?"

Anything with the sound "gyn" in it would perk up people's ears. Dove looked over her shoulder. What looked to be an entire football team of boys was gathered around a grandmotherly lady. They were obviously showing her their support in great testosterone-filled numbers. Dove was sure the woman's problem was a lot more devastating than her own.

All eyes were trained on Dove. She tried to curl her body into itself and turned back to Mr. Gorgeous McLoudypants.

Dove whispered quietly, "Yes, that's it. Thank you."

Mr. Fitzwell leaned closer to hear her. "Okay." He seemed to want to engage in some more conversation. "Have you ever used it before? Because it's a little bit different than your regular VAGINAL cream." His voice just carried; it was like he couldn't stop it if he tried.

Dove let her hands grab one another for support. If she didn't have a wall of teenage meat behind her, she would've run. She wasn't exactly sure because her heart was pumping loudly in her ears, but she thought the supportive boys behind her were snickering.

"No, I… haven't used it before." Dove wondered if she could fit in her own purse.

He obviously was quite proud of his extensive knowledge of pharmaceutical products. He decided to spout the difference between "traditional" yeast infection creams and GYNAZULE®.

"You see it's administered with one dose in an APPLICATOR. It's unique because it contains adhesive that will stick to your VAGINAL WALLS, as opposed to running DOWN YOUR LEGS. I think it's called VAGI-GRAB®. But let me check." Mr. Fitzwell ignored the large crowd and clicked away on his computer.

Don't check. Good fucks out loud. DON'T check!

Dove thought the blush she felt on her cheeks might actually give her sunburn. She tried to be savvy. She wanted to be an empowered woman who tossed tampons around like confetti to just anyone, but she wasn't. She could always try.

"Yup. That's it. VAGI-GRAB®. So, Ms. Glitch, any questions?" He turned his interested, trying-to-be helpful, sexy eyes back to her red, red face.

Dove's voice got quieter as she tried to think of something—

anything—to ask. "Um. Is it unscented?"

Mr. Fitzwell squinted as if he could turn up her volume by making his eyes smaller. "I'm not sure. Are you allergic to any types of VAGINAL medicines?"

Dove's mouth talking before her head could shut her up. "Uh… I need to use very gentle soaps because I have sensitive… parts." Her voice was getting higher and higher.

Mr. Fitzwell looked as professional as a brain surgeon. He clearly wanted her to have the correct information. There were definitely stifled chuckles behind her now. Dove was pretty sure her ass was blushing as well. The crack was sweating all on its own, like it was on a super high diving board about to jump.

"Okay, Ms. Glitch GYNAZULE® is not a soap. It will not work if you put it in and then rinse it off in the shower." He patted the prescription paper to emphasize his words.

Oh God. We're talking about me being naked, in the shower with cooter cream. Please world, end. Kill me.

"I know it's not soap. I just… if it's scented… I can't do scented. Flowers and stuff like that. Fruit-flavored soaps make… things… burnish." She could tell from the peeks at his face Mr. Fitzwell had never stepped foot in a bath and lotion store, wanting to try the array of fun fragrances. Nor had he purchased Peppermint Candy shower gel, foamed up his nether regions, and felt like he had dipped them in lava. Dove crossed and uncrossed her legs at the memory.

Mr. Fitzwell seemed concerned. "Okay, just a heads-up. It's definitely not good to put any fruits or plant life near your genitals." He made a V with his hands and formed his own pretend vagina in front of his pants.

Dove covered her eyes and tried to defend herself because now she could hear the sickly older woman beating her supporters with a purse.

Dove's mumbling got louder with her embarrassment. "I don't put weird things down... there. Just make sure that the cream's vagina-scented. Just plain. For vaginas." She kept her eyes on the counter.

Stop saying "vagina," you screaming asshole!

The assistants were cooing and ogling pictures on the computer. Mrs. Pills had obviously forwarded images of her newborn baby to her coworkers at the perfect time for them not to come to Dove's aid. Finally, Mr. Fitzwell asked her for her phone number and birth date.

"You can wait right over there; I'll have this ready in ten minutes. I'm sure the itching is horrendous."

Dove shuffled to the hard purple chairs and grabbed a magazine off the rack to hide behind. From the questions and directions he asked, Mr. Fitzwell was obviously Mrs. Pill's temporary replacement for her maternity leave. Dove peered over the top of her magazine at him. He was stunning and from the way smiled, he almost knew it. His jaw was like a stiff, hard cliff somewhere in Ireland. The kind on postcards. His Adam's apple was like his throat's erection. Dominant. He had the sleeves of his shirt pushed up and his forearms revealed. Veins and muscles. From doing stuff. All kinds of sexy, manly stuff. The assistants fluffed their hair when he wasn't looking and pretended to pinch his butt.

After the football team took care of the lovely grandma, Dove was as alone as one could be in a Save-Mart. Mr. Fitzwell looked over the counter while he was working to see if she was still there. Just before Dove could scurry her gaze away, she saw him look at her magazine and raise his eyebrows in surprise. Dove hadn't thought to check which magazine she was pretending to be reading. She'd just needed a shield to hide behind. She closed it and looked at the cover. It was a copy of *Cosmopolitan* with large print over most of the cover:

MAKE YOUR ORGASMS LOUDER, HARDER AND LONGER!

Dove dropped the magazine like it was a snake that had bitten her.

Fuck you! Crazy lady magazine!

Dove wanted to cry. This was the worst twenty minutes in her entire existence. After all her semiclandestine feminine product acquisitions, she was facing everything she worked to protect herself against. And the drop-dead gorgeous pharmacist had witnessed it all.

He knew her vagina was sensitive to products and that it was itching. Dove contemplated the magazine again. She wondered if she could actually paper cut herself to death while sitting in the waiting area.

Mr. Fitzwell called her name. "Ms. Glitch? Your GYNAZULE® is ready."

She grabbed her purse and stomped over to the counter. He was smiling at her, ready to ring up her purchase. "You might want to grab some probiotics to go with this. Fight the infection from the inside and the outside."

Dove just stood and stared at him. She rarely got angry and certainly not over womanly products with a man, but she'd had enough.

"Listen, Mr. Fitzwell!" She slammed her purse down in front of him, and he blinked in surprise. "For future reference, when a lady hands you a script like that?" She pointed to the crinkly bag he was holding. "Go get one of the assistants to handle it. No one wants to talk about her 'vaginal walls' "—she mimicked his V-shaped hand motion from earlier—"with a *dude!*"

Dove let out a satisfied breath.

I told him. Good for me.

She didn't expect his hurt expression and dejected nodding. His loud voice was quiet, finally.

"Of course, ma'am. I'm very sorry."

He motioned for her to sign the screen in front of her to accept the prescription. She hated the look on his face—like he was a puppy and she had just kicked him. She took the bag from his hands, careful not to touch his beautiful, long fingers. She couldn't leave him all dejected and dragging.

"It's okay. I overreacted. I get mean when I'm embarrassed."

Instead of helping he shook his head and rolled his eyes. "Great job, Fitzwell. Living the dream now, you big fool." He ran a hand through his perfect hair. He was talking to himself.

Dove bit her lip, and he used her pause to explain himself more. "This is my first day as a pharmacist. I just wanted to be really thorough and make sure you were comfortable with the medicine. I did a great job with that, huh?"

She had been angry with him, but now she had compassion. This was his dream, and she was probably the worst customer to have right out of the gate.

Dove smiled at him. "It's okay, Mr. Fitzwell. I think you're going to make a great pharmacist."

He looked at her doubtfully.

"No, really, you will." She reached out and patted his hand to solidify her message.

They both felt the spark—an actual, blue, snapping spark. Dove's wool jacket, combined with the pharmacy rug, had turned her into a walking electrical appliance. They both pulled their hands away from the contact, shaking their fingers.

"Damn!" Mr. Fitzwell stepped a few feet away from the counter and her.

Dove laughed; it was clear nothing here was going to go well.

"Well, I guess you got me back. I hope you feel better soon, Ms. Glitch." He was smiling at her laughter. At least they could end the experience with a bit of joy. His teeth were pearly white and straight, and there was a hint of a dimple. Her uterus swooned.

"Call me Dove. You already know so much about me." She held out her hand formally.

He gave her a huge smile and went about the most awkward handshake of her life. He touched her palm with his first finger. When there was no shock, he flicked her finger to get rid of any latent electricity.

"Ow!" She winced. His thumping forefinger made her fingers curl into her hand.

"Sorry, sorry. I'm making a mess of this, but it's just that I hate shocks." He finally grasped her hand, but it was before she could completely unclamp her fingers, so he wound up shaking her claw.

"I'm Johnson. Thanks for being my first customer and breaking me in."

He seemed like he was about to release her hand when she dropped her prescription bag between them. They both reached for it at the same time and clanked foreheads together like drunken sumo wrestlers.

"Damn it!" Dove staggered backward.

Johnson put his hands to his head, wincing in pain. The assistants tried to stop giggling, but lost their battle. Dove scooped up the bag and backed away from the disastrous transaction.

"Well, Johnson, I might remember nothing at all after that whack, but my head won't forget when you banged me."

Oh, holy piss cushions. I just said he banged me. Like 'sex' bang.

Johnson reached into the little pharmacy refrigerator and pulled out the first bottle he laid his hands on. He pressed it against the slight contusion on his forehead.

He waved in her direction and had clearly missed her verbal faux pas because he was deep in the middle of his own, shouting, "I like to leave a mark when I bang people!" in his too-loud voice.

Dove's last glimpse of him made her smile for hours. To his forehead, as impromptu first aid, he had a bottle, clearly marked in bold letters: Anal Suppository! Keep Cold!

Chapter 2

Figures, Damn it

For days after her horrendous meeting with Mr. Johnson Loudy McSexypus Fitzwell, Dove would stop to just blush from head to toe. Luckily, her yeast infection and UTI cleared up with the meds. She was able to commence life as normal and prayed that her most delicate of organs stayed disease free until Mrs. Pills got back from maternity leave. Dove blushed again at the thought of her own feminine parts.

Back to normal. Officially, on paper, Dove worked as a ticket ripper for the local park's kiddie carousel. She was also in college to be something but had yet to put down a field as a concentration. As soon as she decided who she was definitely going to be, she changed her mind or failed a test. Deciding meant confidence, and they didn't sell that on street corners. This was her second year as a senior, and she was shaping up to stack a third year on top of the other two.

Every so often, her guidance counselor would demand a meeting with her. Ms. Jorish dressed in free-flowing dresses and made her own jewelry. Dove was pretty sure Ms. Jorish wore buckets of perfume so she could try to cover the smell of pot smoke that lingered around her like an aura. Their meeting earlier that day had been dismal.

"Dover, please come in, sweetheart. Lovely to see you. Please, have a seat." Ms. Jorish pushed Dove into a deep beanbag chair.

Dove tried to mumble a correction, "It's Dove. It's Dove. Duh-vuh. But all one syllable."

Ms. Jorish took off her ever-present sunglasses to give Dove a hard stare. "Sweetheart, I need to place you. We have to nail you down. You're a square peg, and I'll hammer you into a round hole soon."

Despite her carefree attitude, Ms. Jorish liked to see her students graduate. Dove's file was looking grubby and lived in.

"Let's talk about the journalism, Dover. Have you firmed that up? How many credits do you have left?" Ms. Jorish collapsed in the other beanbag chair. Her hair flew around her head like someone had turned on a high-powered leaf blower for an instant.

Dove looked around the office, wishing she could avoid answering. "Um. I was doing pretty well, but then I failed to give a really good oral…"

She felt an uncomfortable gas bubble trickle up her esophagus, and Dove cursed herself for loving soda. She guzzled it straight from the can and liked it ice cold. Usually, she tried to find a quiet place to release any leftover consequences from her unhealthy addiction. But not today. Dove pinched her lips together, sealing the evil burp inside. Ms. Jorish waited, but when it was obvious Dove wasn't going to continue her train of thought, the counselor went off on a tangent.

"Oral? Are we talking sex, Dover? Oral sex is sex. I'll tell you what, so many of the kids nowadays get sucked into giving the oral. They don't think of the consequences. Not all penii are cleanly. And if you're too busy having all the sex, you can't concentrate on your work. God knows what kind of STD you can inhale like a vacuum."

Dove's eyes watered as the burp became a painful rock in her throat. Her blush crept up on her, blotchy and obvious.

Please, please don't talk about sex. Oh God, stop the talking. To open her mouth would be to unleash a horrific belch, so Dove just sat. Ms. Jorish obviously took the blush and tears in Dove's eyes as an admission of her promiscuity.

"Hormones'll drive you crazy, Dover. All you'll do is think with your *vagina*." Ms. Jorish gave a deep, animated voice to Dove's privates. "More! More!"

Dove's eyes bugged out. She thought of the thin door to Ms. Jorish's office.

Please, let the hallway be empty.

Ms. Jorish rolled her head around and returned her voice to normal.

"Tell me, Dover, have you taken up any new hobbies? Is there anything you do besides all the oral?" She leaned forward in her beanbag, squishing it noisily around her bottom.

Too much time had passed for Dove to correct the woman about the sex. She'd wanted to say, *"Oral* report*.!, I did poorly on the oral* report!*"*

Dove attempted to speak without moving her lips. "I've learned to knit some scarves. With some pattern."

Safely keeping the hard burp at the back of her throat, Dove was pleased she had conveyed her thoughts.

Ms. Jorish sat for a few minutes tapping her finger against her lips. "I've got it, Dover!" She became exuberant and tried to stand too quickly. The beanbag held firm to the woman's bottom, and Dove had to watch the bizarre performance of Ms. Jorish crawling and flailing around on the floor for a bit before using her desk to drag herself to her feet. She returned to her conversation as though the spectacle hadn't happened at all.

"You"—she pointed between Dove's eyes—"are perfect for a job I just thought of. Sometimes I amaze myself, truly."

Ms. Jorish held out a hand to help Dove up. Instead of assisting her, it just made it more unmanageable to drag her butt out of the beanbag's grasp.

Finally, they were eye to eye. "Dover, my brother's a warden at the Middletown Penitentiary." The counselor held her hands up and made a square with her fingers. "I see you there as an arts and crafts director. For the inmates. We'll combine your love of blow jobs with the knitting!" She tossed up her hands in appreciation of her own genius.

Dove wanted to puke or at least oppose this woman's horrible new plan for her life, but Ms. Jorish was high on her own idea.

She pushed Dove out the door. "Don't worry sweetheart. I'll send your info to him tonight. This'll be perfect." Just before she closed the door in Dove's face, she tried to comfort Dove a bit. "Don't worry, Dover. I won't tell him about the addiction to fellatio. Just say no to penii for a little while if you can!" The woman's voice carried and echoed in the hallway.

Dove thanked her lucky stars that it was empty like she had prayed. She leaned against Ms. Jorish's door and finally released the burp she had been holding down. It was a doozy, and she covered her mouth, worried the counselor would open the door at the noise. As she hurried away from the scene of her bodily-function crime, she rounded the corner to the lobby of the building. She stopped short at the spectacle of thirty other students peering silently up at her from their Downward Dog positions.

The men in the yoga class were smiling in her direction while the women shook their heads in disgust.

Dove mentally reviewed the words they had surely heard Ms. Jorish use just seconds before. And Dove's loud belch. She covered her mouth and tried to apologize.

"I'm sorry… that I'm alive. I'm… leaving… now."

She learned later that the gymnasium where the yoga class was usually held was having the floors refinished. They had to meet in the lobby right next to Ms. Jorish's office for at least a month. And they were quiet motherfuckers.

A fidgety child snapped Dove back to the present moment at her carousel job. He was picking his nose with one hand and holding out his red ticket with the other. She took it carefully from his hand, trying to avoid the boogers, and ripped it in half. In addition to ripping the children's tickets, her other job at the carousel was to make sure they were buckled on the horses.

It sounded like a wonderful job when she had applied. She loved to be outside, and the park was very pretty. The eccentric old man who owned the ride liked the idea of a ticket taker, but the ride really didn't need one. The moms and dads bought the tickets not ten steps from where Dove stood, and they could easily buckle their own kids.

The happy kids were often screaming and kicking when it came time to take them off the ride. She had perfected unraveling their chubby little hands from the gold pole that kept the horses from running free. Unfortunately, there were many times she'd had to clean a horse's tail and intricate saddle when a full diaper had exploded after an excited little tush wiggled in it.

She often found herself with large chunks of empty time on her hands. The owner didn't mind when she pulled out her phone to tweet. He mistakenly thought Dove was working on her class papers on her "newfangled, super tiny keyboard." She didn't bother to correct him because on Twitter, she was someone else.

Dove loved to see her sexy icon on the screen. It was mostly boobs. On Twitter she never burped or mumbled or had vaginal itching.

She was @Lotsa_Vampersex there. And she was witty on the Twitty. She was up to four hundred followers who watched her tweets with baited breath. Lotsa found herself in achingly sexy situations in her pretend life and she tweeted about it often. Dove gave a little tweet just to see them get excited.

***Lotsa Vampersex** (@Lotsa_Vampersex):*
Licking an ice pop slowly in my sheer, white teddy.

She was 140 characters of awesome, every single damn time. She scrolled happily through her @'s as the followers trickled in.

***Hotdaddy3_6** (@Hotdaddy3):*
@Lotsa_Vampersex tell me more Lotsa!

One after another, they reminded her that she mattered, and she liked it. She checked the clock on her cell phone and closed the ride for her brief lunch break. She waved at Marge, the ticket seller, who was knee-deep in a bodice ripper romance book by Debra Anastasia and ignored Dove completely.

Dove found a seat overlooking the pond and took out a yogurt from her large, monogrammed bag. She hated how big it was, but her cute, kitschy lime green lunch sack was home airing out. Her pickle had exploded out of its watery pouch last week, and Dove had no idea how to clean it.

Not every day needs to smell like pickles.

Her large, navy one was big enough to support all the side dishes required for a huge family reunion.

She'd just scooped a big spoonful of vanilla yogurt into her mouth when she felt the wood of the bench creak its disapproval at the added weight of another person. She looked to her left shoulder and almost spit out the contents of her mouth. Her cheeks were full like a chipmunk's as she took in the sight of her loud, gorgeous, temporary pharmacist.

He smiled at her and exclaimed, "GYNAZULE®!"

He pounded her on the back like an old friend, and Dove had to work to keep her yogurt in her mouth.

"Eating some yogurt? That's great for your VAGINAL health. Good bacteria and all." He seemed to take her distressed look as a reprimand and made a face. "Sorry. Vaginal health," he stage-whispered in a seeming reaction to her tirade at the pharmacy.

She'd recovered enough from her shock and was just about to swallow when Johnson decided to become concerned.

"Are you going to throw up?" He looked intensely into her eyes.

He's beautiful.

She shook her head furiously.

Just swallow, you dumbass.

"You're choking? Oh God." Johnson launched into action with fervor.

He jumped up and stood in front of her. "They taught us this. Stay calm. I know the Heimlich."

If Dove could have screamed, she would have; instead, she became a floppy rag doll as Johnson yanked her from her sitting position. She tried to wave him off and tell him with her eyes to just give her a motherfucking second to swallow. But he assumed the position behind her and accidentally grabbed her boobs while lining up his hands under her ribs.

She heard his embarrassed but determined voice in her ear.

"Sorry about that. Hang on, Gynazule®."

He was exceptionally forceful, and the Heimlich works for a reason. Dove was forced to expel her yogurt all over her stadium-sized lunch sack. A small crowd of joggers and moms pushing strollers had stopped to watch the struggle with the intense curiosity of rubberneckers.

He was still jerking her all around before she could holler, *"Put me down! I was eating! Not choking! Damn it!"*

Johnson set her down and whirled her around. "Airway, good. Breathing, good. Circulation, good." He ignored the crowd and focused on her face. "Are you okay?"

Dove wiped her mouth and slapped her thigh. "Yes. I was swallowing my yogurt. I wasn't choking. And my name's Dove, not GYNAZULE®."

Understanding hit Johnson on the top of his head, and he looked disgusted with himself. "Man, I just can't get anything right. I'm so sorry, Dove."

She sighed and turned to the gawkers. "Move along. Haven't you seen a girl hurl yogurt before?" She motioned at them in anger. "Unless you're all going help me clean it up?"

The crowd began to disperse. Some were laughing; some looked grossed out. Johnson took a handkerchief from his pocket and headed for her sack. He had every intention of using his fancy linen to clean up her spew.

"No, Fitzwell. Stop." She grabbed the sack and tossed it in the nearby trashcan. "These things are impossible to clean."

He stuck his hands in his pockets. He looked adorable without his lab coat. His perfectly pleated pants and tie were obviously expensive. She collapsed on the next bench over and held her head in her hands. She felt him sit next to her.

His super-loud voice was slightly softer as he tried to

apologize again. "Why do I do the stupidest stuff around you?"

More than her frustration with him bubbled to the top, and she decided to vent. "You know why? Because I'm a sucking hole of failure. My job? I collect tickets from shit-filled kids. My career? According to my cracked-out guidance counselor, I should be giving blow jobs to felons in jail in between teaching them to knit. I keep being in the wrong place, doing the wrong thing, at the wrong freaking time. I suck at being a human."

She risked a glance at his handsome face. He squinted at the horizon, the sun picking up the blond highlights in his hair. He looked like he might say something that would ease her mind. Instead: "I really think it's a bad idea to bring knitting needles into jail."

He turned to look at her in earnest.

"Oh, for crap's sake. I'm not teaching in jail!" She stomped her feet in front of her, causing little dust clouds to form around her shoes.

He put his hand on hers. "Hey, Dove, I'm kidding."

And he was. He was smiling at her despite her lousy job. He was smiling at her even though he knew she had vaginal problems.

"Good. Because I may've had to beat the crap out of you if you weren't." She let him keep his hand in hers, enjoying the attention of a real, non-Twitter man.

The two sat quietly on the park bench, and Dove liked it. If she sat perfectly still, neither could ruin the moment. He seemed to feel the change as well as they watched two squirrels bound about in front of them.

The squirrels were adorable and brave, jumping close to Dove and Johnson—maybe because they were motionless.

Dove wanted to comment on the Disneyesque scene in front

of them but kept her words on the tip of her tongue, not wanting to spoil the quiet. The two squirrels sat side by side, each a mirror of the other, munching on acorns in their paws. With their fuzzy faces and sweet, black eyes, they reminded Dove of exactly why she loved the park. Next to her, Johnson sighed in contentment.

The male squirrel dropped his nut and jumped quickly behind the female squirrel.

Oh dear God! Don't do it. You horny little bastard!

The male squirrel refused to read Dove's mind and started climbing on the female squirrel.

Dove heard Johnson's groan of disgust as the male began the motions of copulation. She shook her head.

Fucking figures.

The tender new feelings between Dove and this handsome man were now spoiled with the obscene visual of the hairy rodents humping.

Chapter 3

The Cooler

Johnson had to comment. "Wow. Squirrels usually engage in some style of MATING dance." He looked around the park for other examples to prove his point. "Much like humans, they're attracted to the smell of the GENITALS and fancy tail motions."

Dove tried to figure out where she belonged in this conversation that he apparently thought was acceptable small talk. The obscene, public intercourse ended with one final, furry pump. The female never even dropped her nut.

"Well, I guess that was a dinner date." Dove covered her mouth and shook her head. She prayed for a flock of hungry hawks to swoop in and eat the little Snow White porn stars so she and Mr. Gorgeouspants could just stop talking about nether regions for a minute.

"This time of the year, NUTS are more important than anything else. To a squirrel, that is." Johnson played with his tie in a way that told Dove he had hardly worn one before.

He seemed to be deep in thought before an idea hit him. "Oh. Your lunch! You had to throw it out because of me! Can I buy you something?"

Dove thought of throwing her cell phone at the Chip 'n' Dale imposters in front of them. The boy was getting a twinkle in his eye again. His fat-assed girlfriend would never run when she was having a nut chow down. She would take it like the whore she was.

"Um. I have to get back to the ride. My break's like fifteen minutes." Dove checked her phone out of habit.

"No. Look, there's a hot dog stand over there. I'll be right back." He was up and crossing the grass purposefully before Dove could tell him to stop. She slid her phone back into her pocket.

Weiner Wonderland was wheeled into the park at ten thirty in the morning and wheeled out at nine thirty at night. Sal never changed his gloves once in all that time. He never left to use the bathroom, either. To the ladies who purchased his hot dogs, he would always hand them over with a sneer. He watched them eat and licked his lips as if they were latching onto his penis instead of processed meat.

Dove never, ever ate a dog from his cart. If she did indulge in a tube steak, it was in her own apartment, on a hot dog bun with nothing on it. Plain, plain, plain. She hated to have any food on her plate touch one another. Soon enough, Johnson was headed back to her with a soda and Sal's wiener with *everything* on it.

Sal was wiggling his one, long unibrow, licking his lips in anticipation of her mouth coming in contact with his meat. Dove's stomach rolled at the thought of even putting the oily hot dog in her hands.

Johnson had a huge gait, like he was stepping over little towns of fairies and it brought him back to her with his prize quickly. Dove looked at the ominous dog. It was sloppy—piled high with relish, mustard, ketchup, and some brown chunks Sal insisted was chili.

"I didn't know what you like, so I got you everything." Johnson extended the dog to her.

"That's a great policy when you're shopping in a jewelry store. Not so much for Sal and his wieners." Dove cringed but accepted the meat.

Johnson looked crestfallen. "Look at me—mistake after mistake. I can't get it right."

Dove hated to see him dejected. "No, it's great. I'm starving. Ejecting the contents of my stomach has really brought out the bear in me."

She lifted the hot dog to her mouth and tried not to smell it. In her peripheral vision, she saw Sal put his gloved hands down his pants. She snapped off a small bite and chewed as quickly as she could.

Johnson popped the top of her soda and held it out to her like a gentleman. She guzzled the cold soda to wash away the traces of the meat down her hatch.

"I'm glad you're eating, I was afraid I had ruined your lunch." Johnson rubbed his hands together, smiling at her.

"This is so much better than nothing. No, really. I love penis-shaped meat." Dove tried to gag down another bite but switched to more soda.

Stop saying penis, you fart fruit.

"You hate it. I'm a jerk. What time do you get off? I need to make this up to you." He sat down next to her.

Dove wondered if this was the pharmacist asking her on a date. @Lotsa_Vampersex would've started gyrating and popping buttons off her shirt.

But Dove was reserved. "I get off around seven. I have to wipe down the horses."

Johnson looked over at the carousel. "You have to groom the fake horses?"

Dove tried not to look at the oozing hot dog. Sal was dry-humping his hot dog cart. Again.

"No, I have to antibacterial them. Children are filthy." She bit her lip.

Now she sounded like a child racist. Or an age racist. Or some withered-ovary shrew.

"Children are germ carriers." He seemed to be trying to continue her odd train of thought.

Dove sought to ease the tension with another bite of the meat. Johnson grimaced as the toppings dripped down her chin. She wiped them off with her sleeve.

Sal's humping reached a fever pitch. Johnson looked over his shoulder to see what was causing the banging-on-metal noise.

After witnessing the spectacle, he turned back to Dove. She had downed another huge gulp of her drink, hoping whatever corrosive acid in soda that rots teeth in minutes would also kill the festering germs Sal had added to her dog.

"Do you think that vendor'll be okay?" Johnson ran a hand through his perfect hair.

Dove's punishment for her turbo drinking was another epic burp. She refused to release it.

Better to have it go out the back than out the mouth.

Dove tried to find a solution. "Yeah, he'll be all right. He has groinal seizures?"

Did I just say that out loud?

The medical nerd in Johnson perked up. "Really? I wonder if that's a side effect of any medicines he's taking."

He got lost in his contemplation. Marge was waving at Dove with her horrible romance novel. There was a crappy-looking little kid holding a red ticket.

"Well, thanks for the lunch. I've got to go do my thing." Dove thought it'd be rude to throw away the hot dog with only two bites taken out of it.

She juggled her soda so she could hold out her hand.

Johnson stood and gave her a forceful shake. "I'll be back at seven. Thanks, Dove, for not pressing charges or anything about the whole yogurt incident."

"You, too. Okay. Later. Bye." You, too? What the hell am I saying?

Dove rushed back to her spot by the gate and set her gift hot dog from Johnson down on her little folding chair.

The crappy child held his ticket up to her while staring with his big, blue, blinky eyes. He had the chubby cheeks of good health. Dove hated the chubby cheeks; in her experience, those little bastards filled their diapers every third breath.

Without fail, his mother took a shaky, unfocused cell phone picture of Cheeks and waved at him every single time he came around on the ride. Dove didn't like how the hot dog kept repeating itself, battling with the soda for the dominance of her tongue.

Little Chubs McShitty had indeed honked one off on the horse. Luckily, his pants held in his mess. He began the epic fling, fly, cry when Dove put his little feet by the exit. The mother thanked her and called the awful stench "stinky poopy poos," which didn't make it smell any less like a drunk trucker just took a man-sized dump in the direct vicinity. After the little bastard left with his mom, Dove spent the rest of her time tweeting and contemplating her date with Mr. Fitzwell.

I mean, it had to be a date, right?

She decided to tease her Twitter followers:

Lotsa Vampersex *(@Lotsa_Vampersex):*
Don't get jealous. I have a date tonight. Don't worry, I'll still be dreaming of u.

The ride had very few customers. Dove eventually threw out her hot dog because the flies were starting to make the unappetizing thing look even worse. She tried to avoid looking at Sal because he'd take a limp dog and wiggle it in her direction when he caught her eye.

Never again, Sal. Never again.

Dove dipped into her purse and refreshed her lip gloss and fluffed her hair. It was now six forty-five and Johnson would be back soon. She wished she had time to go back and put her nice underwear on.

Get real, Dove. You haven't had a date that didn't involve a keyboard in…

She sighed when she realized she wasn't exactly sure she was smart enough to do the math on that one.

It's better this way. No time to get all anal and second-guess myself.

She got a horrible stomach cramp.

Stupid Sal. That hot dog's going through me like a freight train.

Dove felt the traveling gas bubble that her soda addiction often gave her.

Damn it. I better pop this one off before Johnson shows up. Don't want it to still be lingering when he arrives.

Another sharp cramp made her grab her stomach.

Oh. No.

She began feeling the feverish chills.

If that fucker gave me food poisoning, I'll drown him in that hot dog water.

The gas bubble competed with the cramps for mastery of her anus.

This isn't going to be good.

Dove gave a small push hoping for a tiny fart and was alarmed at the forceful boom from her bottom. She was about to tell Marge that she was going to have to cut out early when she unlocked her phone and Twitter came up on her screen. Out of habit, she checked her replies. The boys were sad she had a date. She loved toying with them.

Johnson's voice caused her to jump and fart at the same time. She was hoping her little scream of surprise drowned out the unladylike noise.

He was in front of her, finishing his sentence, so she tried to tune in.

"…you do the Twitter? So do I. What's your handle? I'm new at it. I just picked my birthday and combined them with my favorite drug. I love numbers."

He was talking and laughing while holding the handle of a huge cooler on wheels.

I sharted when he scared me. Oh my God. Kill me.

Dove tried to pretend that she hadn't just shit her pants. Johnson hadn't noticed. He was still happy to have a Twitter connection to her.

"My Twitter is @06201984M358. I know, right? Who can remember that?" He stood there shaking his head.

Dove stood stock-still; she didn't want to stir anything up. But it was only a matter of time before it was very, very obvious something foul was afoot.

Or ashit.

"Well, sorry I'm a little early. I have a problem with worrying whether or not my clock's right. Sometimes when I wear these pants, my watch goes a bit slower."

He smiled to reveal glamorous teeth. When she didn't respond, he shrugged.

"Do you smell that? Oh God, it's awful." He wrinkled his nose in disgust.

Dove gave him the first lie she could think of. "A crappy kid crapped his pants." She tried to curl her shoulders around her face.

"Well, that's what crappy kids do. It's still lingering. That's one ripe kid."

Dove felt her panties squish. Another cramp reared its head, wanting to burst out seeing that her digestive system had gotten started.

"He was disgusting. Children are the devil."

Go away beautiful man. Just walk away.

He raised his eyebrow at her harsh statement. "You're rough on the kids, huh? Well, anyway. I bought you a new cooler. Look, it has wheels. I noticed how big your last one was, so I upgraded you. You could fit the hugest lunch in here!"

He dragged it around like a dog on a leash. The cooler was humongous. Dove tried not to move.

"Man, that stench is just hanging here like a fiend, right?" Johnson waved his hand in front of his face.

Dove nodded.

"Okay. Well, just wanted to drop this off and apologize again. I better get going. Thanks a lot for being here. At your job. I'm going to run, 'cause honestly, that smell's making me nauseous."

Dove nodded and waved. He waited for her to say more, but she just covered her face with her hand. Soon she heard his retreating steps. He didn't want a date; he wanted to give her the biggest cooler in existence. She'd crapped her pants and acted like a baby-hating, nonverbal, ungrateful, stinky bitch.

This is really where a meteor could fall on my head, and I'd be okay with that. They could even use this cooler as my coffin.

And don't miss Fire in the Hole which is the sequel to Fire Down Below. It is also out NOW and enrolled in Kindle Unlimited.

Other Titles By Debra Anastasia

New Adult:

Poughkeepsie Begins
Poughkeepsie
Return to Poughkeepse
Saving Poughkeepsie
*Enhanced Interactive Poughkeepsie for iPads, mobiles
and Computers for FREE*

Felony Ever After

#1 Amazon Humor Bestseller:

Fire Down Below
Fire in the Hole

Booty Call

Paranormal:

Crushed Seraphim
Bittersweet Seraphim

Dark Romance:

The Revenger

100% proceeds donated to Save the Tatas:

Late Night with Andres

Upcoming Debra Anastasia Titles:

New Adult:

For All The Evers (Fall 2016)

Everlock (Spring 2017)

Comedy:

Cherry Farts (Winter 2016)

Made in the USA
Columbia, SC
05 August 2019